DIMINISHED, RESOLVING TO MAJOR

DIMINISHED, RESOLVING TO MAJOR

A Novel By

ROBERT HAUS

EMPRESS

PUBLICATIONS

WWW.EMPRESSPUBLICATIONS.COM

For Heather Flower
1979-2020

PART ONE

Hollywood

I

The pianist watched the orchestra conductor with a keen eye. But the conductor didn't even glance at the orchestra. Wearing headphones, he led the orchestra through a harsh piece of music while giving his full attention to a movie playing on a large screen behind the musicians. The upbeats and downbeats of his baton moved in synch with the violent action on the screen. The conductor barely glanced at the music score. The pianist knew why. The conductor was also the composer, and obviously knew every note of the score.

The pianist and the other musicians couldn't see the screen, but they had no need. Each kept one eye on the music score in front of them and the other eye on the man with the baton.

This was the pianist's first film score gig. He knew the conductor/composer, a brown-haired man in his thirties named Ed, was one of the most in-demand film score composers in Hollywood. The pianist burned with determination to make a good impression with both Ed and the other musicians. If he earned their approval, it could lead to more such gigs, and—he dared to hope—a steady income.

You're performing with some of the most legendary musicians in Hollywood, he thought. *This is NOT the time to screw up!*

He fought the temptation of nervousness and forced himself to focus on the music. His position near the back of the orchestra was not his usual vantage point. For this gig, he functioned as an anonymous member of the percussion section. Ed and his conductor's podium seemed distant, on the far side of a forest of musicians, black music stands, and a seemingly haphazard arrangement of microphones, with the mike stands bent at various rakish angles.

The orchestra sounded as if it were staggering under a musical load of harsh, savage pounding and vertigo-inducing gyrations. The bows of the violinists and cellists moved back and forth in perfect, ballet-like synchronization. Ed raised his hands above his head for the upbeat, then cued the pianist on the downbeat.

The pianist played a violent two-bar phrase. His left hand remained stationary, near the middle of the keyboard, while his right hand descended in a spiky riff that sounded like shattering glass. He played the riff flawlessly and – just for a moment – permitted himself an inner smile. Ed led the orchestra through one last phrase, this one softer and less violent, then held the next-to-last chord, an intense E-Diminished, for several long moments before finally resolving to a relaxed F-Major.

After holding the last chord for several moments, Ed gave the cutoff with his hands held out, the signal for silence. It wasn't really necessary. The musicians were all pros. They remained silent for a good five seconds after the cutoff.

Ed let his hands fall, removed his headphones and said, "Thank you all. Let's take fifteen, then come back for the end titles." He disappeared into the booth to review the recording with the film director and the studio engineer.

The pianist pivoted on the piano bench and faced the screen on the rear wall of the recording studio. After a few moments, a film clip lit up the screen. The just-recorded music emanated from within the booth. On the screen, two men fought each other atop a building overlooking downtown LA. The pianist permitted himself another inner smile as he heard the spiky riff he'd just played match the action of one man knocking the other out. Then he heard the final two chords, Diminished to Major, as a beautiful young woman dashed into the victorious man's muscular arms.

Ed reappeared from the booth and crossed over to the pianist. Like everyone else in the orchestra, he wore the casual attire of studio musicians – in his case, jeans and a light green polo shirt. He offered the pianist his hand and said, "Nice work. Appreciate you taking this on such short notice."

"My pleasure. Good to meet you. I hope Ben gets over the flu soon."

"How long have you been in LA?"

"Almost two years."

"Doing okay?" Ed asked, with an almost imperceptible note of softness in his baritone voice.

The pianist replied with care.

"Okay. Plenty of good pianists out there."

Ed gave him a sympathetic grin and said, "Well, you showed up on time. And sober. With little notice. That puts you ahead of the pack. Could I get your card?"

"Sure!" He fished into his wallet and pulled out a business card. Ed took it and said, "Great. Thanks again."

The pianist was elated. Ed was thanking HIM? This was a red-letter day, his first film score recording session, and it was damn near perfect. He turned in a flawless performance. He met and worked with some of LA's legendary studio musicians. And he pleased Ed, who was known in LA music circles as a really good guy, someone always willing to help struggling young musicians.

After the recording session ended, the pianist drove his '63 Ford Falcon Ranchero pickup through the hot, late afternoon Los Angeles sun to the Hollywood post office. He collected his meager mail and cruised down Vine Street to the Musicians Union. Once inside, he deposited his check at the Musicians Credit Union ATM, transferring more than half to his savings account. Then he scanned the bulletin boards and saw job announcements for violinists, guitarists, and drummers.

Nothing of interest today.

He spotted some acquaintances in the lobby and chatted them up. He mentioned the day's film score session and could tell they were impressed. That was good. Other musicians knew he was working, at least today. It was the conundrum of the musician's life – if you were seen as working, and hirable, more gigs came your way. If you weren't getting any gigs, people assumed there was a reason, and your phone rang rarely, if at all.

Often, there were reasons. Some of the musicians who tried to work in LA just weren't good enough. Some had talent, but also had egos that matched or exceeded their abilities. As Ed hinted, some had poor work habits. Others had substance abuse issues or other problems that derailed their otherwise-promising careers.

The pianist had a problem, too, but he did all he could to hide it from everyone, musician and non-musician alike.

He drove out of the Musicians Union parking lot, up Vine Street, then made a right onto Santa Monica Boulevard, where he reached an ARCO gas station. They had a deal some union members wryly called "the musician's power lunch" – two hot dogs for 99 cents. The pianist bought two, along with a bag of peanuts, an apple, and a copy of the LA Times. Then he asked for the key to the men's room. He set the food on the seat of his car and picked up a steel canteen. Once inside the men's room, he filled the canteen with water from the sink.

Back in his car, he contemplated the question he asked himself every evening, the question that always brought a sour feeling to his stomach. *Where to now?* Finding a place to park his car, and to sleep without being hassled, was the toughest part of his current life. You might be able to find a quiet side street in a residential neighborhood, but it was tricky. Shopping centers were deserted at night, but a lone vehicle was too obvious. He'd slept for a couple of nights in a library parking lot. But a policeman rapped him awake one morning. He got by with just a warning, and never returned. Night after night he slept with one eye open, hoping no one would roust him awake with rough raps on his windshield, or break into his car while he was sleeping, pull a gun, and take what little he had.

Above all, he wanted to avoid parking his car anywhere in the San Fernando Valley. Most of the working musicians lived in the Valley. He did not want to run the risk of another musician spotting him sleeping in his car.

This night was different from most. He'd picked up a good-sized check from the recording session and could afford to splurge. For a moment, he considered a motel, but decided even the cheapest were too pricey. Instead, he opted for the long-term parking lots at LAX. Nothing at all suspicious about a car – one of many – left overnight in one of those lots. Besides, the price wasn't too bad if you stayed only one night. It was worth it to get a night of almost-guaranteed uninterrupted sleep. The money he saved would go into his savings, and, he hoped, toward his goal of six months of rent for an apartment, or even a decent room.

He took the usual route – west on Santa Monica Boulevard, toward the setting Los Angeles sun. Then south on the San Diego freeway, which, as usual, was packed solid with cars during the evening commute. He spent an hour inching south, until he finally came to the exit for the first of many long-term airport parking lots.

He pulled into the first lot, took the ticket and drove down several rows, until he found a space between an enormous pickup with a camper shell and a full-sized van. His little Ford Falcon pickup practically disappeared between the two massive vehicles, which was exactly what he wanted. He chowed down on the hot dogs, the apple, and the peanuts, then read his mail and the LA Times. Harrison Ford's new movie, an updated version of "The Fugitive" TV show, got a rave review. The new president, Bill Clinton, was taking heat from the Republicans. The pianist knew that Clinton played jazz tenor saxophone. He was pulling for Clinton.

By the time he finished reading the paper, dusk had fallen on the parking lot. As so often happened, a wave of depression washed over him. The desolate parking lot resembled an asphalt desert – lifeless, impersonal, and, despite the Los Angeles sun – cold. The sight and sound of airliners taking off and landing, each full of happy people who could afford the air fare, who were flying off to business meetings or vacations or family get-togethers … and his life was reduced to this, to sleeping inside a thirty-year old Ford.

Been almost seven months, now. Never thought it would last this long. Don't know how much more of this I can take.

He forced the depression aside.

Enough of that. Stop feeling so goddam sorry for yourself. You had a good day, getting hired for a film score and earning a healthy paycheck. That check will go a long way toward the goal. Stop whining and get yourself more gigs like that one, and you won't have to live like this any longer.

He covered the windshield, the side windows and the rear window with cardboard sun screens. He yawned and reached for the threadbare blanket that covered the seat backs, pulled it up to his shoulders and wound it around his torso. The pianist lay flat on the seat, his head on the passenger side and his legs folded, and was asleep within minutes.

His watch beeped him awake at 5:30. He sat up, his joints feeling much stiffer than any twenty-six-year-old's should have felt. After rubbing his face for a moment, he discreetly pulled down the cardboard sunscreens, one by one. No signs of security guards out the windshield. Or the right window. Or the left window. Or the rear. He removed the shields, folded them, and stored them behind the seat. He started the engine, put the little Ford in gear and drove to the exit gate. After paying the fee, he threaded his way onto the northbound San Diego Freeway and toward another day in LA.

About three miles before the 405/101 interchange, he noticed something odd – a full-sized Dodge pickup truck parked on the shoulder of the 405. Two men stood on the right-hand side of the truck and took turns heaving several pieces of lumber out of the truck bed and down the embankment. His engineer father would have been appalled at the sight of all that perfectly good lumber going to waste. Soon, the truck and the men disappeared in the Ford's rearview mirror, and the pianist turned his attention to his day ahead.

He took the connecting ramp to the westbound U.S. Route 101, the Ventura Freeway, and headed toward his first stop – the gym near his old apartment in Reseda. The gym was his lifeline, which often struck him as more than a bit ironic. He, who had despised gym class all through junior high and high school, now valued his gym membership above anything except his musician's union card. The membership, a gift from his sister, provided an outlet for his emotions, that was for certain. He worked off tremendous amounts of frustration and anger with the exercycles and weights. And it offered one more benefit, one almost beyond value – the showers.

Every day, sometimes twice a day, he showered at the gym and thanked God for the chance to remain clean and presentable. Without the gym's showers, he would look no different from the filthy vagrants who lined the streets beneath the freeway overpasses, who earned sneers and scowls from passersby, and who often received harsh rebukes from those asked for a handout.

The pianist knew that, although he was homeless, he was not in the same category as the street denizens. But he also knew that if he ever stood a chance of climbing out of his current situation, he could not afford to look even a little bit like them. He had to keep up appearances.

He exited the Ventura Freeway and drove along the surface streets until he arrived at the gym. Once inside, he changed into his workout clothes and pedaled the stationary bicycle for a good fifteen minutes, gradually increasing the resistance. Then he spent 45 minutes at the various weight contraptions, forcing himself to press and pull and flex until his muscles screamed in protest. The pain and the labored breathing felt like a form of penance, the just punishment for the lousy mess he'd gotten himself into.

Finally, after an hour, he made his way to his reward, the luxury of all luxuries – the hot shower. He stayed in the shower for about twenty minutes, scrubbing himself clean. After toweling off, he took a prudent look around the shower area. He was, thankfully, alone, and brushed his teeth in one of the sinks. That could be a dead giveaway, and he knew he had to be careful. Once or twice, one of the other gym members had called him on it. *Hey pal, can't you brush your teeth at home?* He told them he'd just finished either breakfast or lunch and just needed a quick once-over. Most of the time, they seemed to believe him. Shaving was another matter. Rather than shaving at the sinks, he kept his beard trimmed by ducking into the toilet stalls, locking the door and snipping the hairs of his beard with a small pair of scissors and a hand mirror.

With the workout and shower finished, he headed out to the parking lot. Just as he settled into the driver's seat of his car, two more of his lifelines came into play – his pager and his cell phone. Both were just beginning to gain popularity among musicians and other LA freelancers. Like his gym membership, his pager and cell phone were gifts.

His engineer father, unlike many other men his age, had never been put off by modern technology. Just the opposite. His father wanted the latest and best of everything, and was among the first to own one of the early "brick" cellphones, even though they cost a fortune and didn't have much to offer in the way of either performance or convenience. When the second generation of "clamshell phones" hit the market, his father immediately bought one and handed the "brick" off to the pianist. Two weeks after his father died, the pianist received the clamshell phone in the mail. With no place to live, the pianist relied on his pager and cell for gigs.

Now his pager buzzed, with the phone number for his drummer friend Skip showing in the readout. He picked up his cell and dialed the number.

"Hello?" a familiar male voice answered.

"Hey, Skip. What's up?"

"Lots. Listen, can you be at the union at 11:00?"

"Sure."

"Here's the thing," Skip said. "I've been playing in a trio with Chucky Betts, the comedian. Know him?"

"Heard of him."

"He just started performing with a trio two months ago. Added singing to his standup comedy. Moo Cowley was playing piano, but the two of them got into a shouting match last night. We need a new pianist, fast. Only three more gigs for now, but there could be more in the future."

"I'll be there," the pianist replied, trying to sound calm and casual. "Can Betts actually sing?"

"He can carry a tune," Skip replied.

"Good. Thanks. See you at eleven." He hung up his phone, started the engine and headed to the 101.

About five miles in, he spotted some debris on the road. He wasn't sure what it was — wood, metal, or plastic. He wanted to swerve, but an eighteen-wheeler occupied the lane to his left, while a van boxed him in to the right. He braced and felt the tires hit the debris, and hoped for no damage.

No such luck. He felt the car pulling to the left, and soon heard and felt the *rump-rump-rump* of a flat tire. It felt like the driver's side front tire. He signaled to change lanes to the right. The van moved ahead. But he saw an enormous pickup several feet behind the van.

As soon as he started to change lanes, the pickup driver sounded his horn. Instead of slowing down to make room for a car with a flat, the pickup driver sped up, trying to cut him off.

Move back to the center!

Too late, the eighteen-wheeler had already moved into the center lane. The pickup hit his horn again, then screeched his brakes.

Damn it! Over to the shoulder! Now!

The pickup filled all three of his mirrors. He waited for the impact. The two vehicles came close. But at the last moment, he eased his way onto the right shoulder. The pickup sped past, the horn still blaring, the driver shouting, "ASS HOLE!"

Hands shaking, he drove the Ford along the sound wall-lined shoulder and then down the first exit ramp, the lame tire rump-rumping. The steering wheel quivered. The ramp's shoulder ended at an intersection with a local cross street. He pulled the Ford off the ramp with care, limped into a strip mall parking lot and shut the engine off.

"Damn it!" he shouted, out of anger and relief. The pickup driver was typical of so many he encountered on LA freeways. When they saw someone trying to change lanes, they refused to let the person in. Instead, they immediately sped up and tried to cut the other person off. Normally, it was just obnoxious. But when the other vehicle is disabled and trying to get off the road, that sort of behavior was damn dangerous.

And the guy had the nerve to call ME an asshole! Sheesh! How many other drivers like the pickup jockey were out there? It was a miracle more people weren't killed on LA's freeways.

He opened his door, exited the car, and got a look at the front tire. It was flat and smelled of hot rubber, but at least the bead wasn't broken. He decided to let the tire cool off for a few minutes, then see if his can of fix-a-flat would work.

The close call, and the Santa Ana winds that howled across the street and the freeway, left him sweating. The Santa Anas came out of the east, out of the desert. Hot and dry, they could, in an instant, turn the smallest spark into a raging firestorm. Their one saving grace – they blew the ugly smog out of the basin, out to the sea, giving LA residents a brief glimpse of what the city looked like back in the days when achingly clear blue skies reigned over the Southland. Longtime Los Angelenos told him the smog wasn't as bad as it had once been, but it was still bad enough to frequently obscure the nearby San Gabriel mountains in a grey shroud.

As his pulse returned to normal, he noticed something odd across the street. The freeway on-ramp stood next to a church parking lot, with a chain-link fence next to the lot. Tall trees and slightly smaller bushes stood between the fence and the on-ramp's sound wall, with a chained gate connecting the wall and the fence.

Several harsh gusts of the Santa Anas battered the vegetation. The last gusts were so violent, they bent the bushes at a sharp angle, revealing a large open area between the bushes and the trees. Then the winds calmed down, and the bushes once again covered up the open space.

Interesting. I'll bet most people pass by the on-ramp and parking lot all day long with no idea the open space even exists. The walls and bushes do a good job of hiding it from the view of passing drivers and churchgoers. I've seen my share of poorly covered bald spots during my time in Hollywood. More than a few middle-aged men would feel quite a bit of envy for this site.

He turned his attention back to the flat tire. After retrieving the can of fix-a-flat from beneath the seat, he connected it to the valve stem and pressed the cap tab. The flat tire inflated. He kept the tab pressed down until the stream of air and fluid slowed to a halt.

Okay, twenty psi. Drive for a few miles to spread the gluey gunk around the inside of the tire, then find a gas station with an air hose.

He fired up the engine, put the Falcon in gear, and headed back onto the freeway.

After a several minutes, he took the Lankershim exit in Studio City and found a gas station with an air hose. He plugged the hose into the valve stem, heard first the *whissh* and then the *whirr* of the passing air and inflated the tire to the full 32 psi.

Lucked out on that one. He had a spare tire, but it was iffy. Even if he had to use it, he still would have had to buy a new tire. "Never EVER be caught without a spare tire," his father had lectured. "If you have to choose between food and tires, go with tires!" Lucky or not, he decided to spend the money for a new tire as soon as possible. Hard to say how long the fix-a-flat would hold the damage.

Basking in the glow of his good fortune, he decided to splurge – he walked into the gas station's enclosure and bought a bottle of cranberry-grape juice. After paying for the juice, he checked his watch. 9:30. Plenty of time to get to the union.

Let's take our time and enjoy the drink for a change. At that moment, another gust of oven-like Santa Ana winds battered him.

Across the street, near the freeway on ramp, he noticed a parked Highway Patrol car with flashing lights. The CHP officer escorted a man who looked utterly squalid – wild gray hair, unwashed reddish-tan skin, and soiled clothes. Even worse, he seemed to have a vacant, blown-fuse look in his eyes. The CHP officer didn't bother to arrest the man. He just forced him to pick up his tent and sleeping bag and move on.

I feel for you, man. But maybe you need to be a bit less conspicuous. Find someplace to camp out that's not as …

Another harsh Santa Ana breeze battered the pianist. He stood, stock-still, for a long moment.

People pass by that on-ramp all day long with no idea the open space even exists! That's it! Let's check it out, now!

No, not now. Get to the Union. LA traffic can be capricious. Don't blow this gig by being late.

With some reluctance, he started the Ford and made his way to the Musician's Union.

He thanked himself for allowing extra time. An accident blocked several lanes of the eastbound 101, backing up traffic. The Falcon had no radio, leaving him with no access to traffic reports. He made it to the union at 10:30.

Once inside, he checked the bulletin boards, chatted with a few friends, then found the rehearsal room Skip had reserved. He said hello to Skip and Fred, the bass player. Skip introduced him to Chucky Betts, the comedian and the source of his next paycheck.

Betts stood about five-ten, with black hair, blue eyes, and the stocky build of a halfback. Betts squeezed the pianist's hand with as much force as possible. The pianist tacitly cursed the people who long ago decreed bone-cracking grips to be indisputable proof of honesty and macho-manliness.

Along with his comedy and singing, Betts also played guitar. To keep things above-board, he joined the union and tried to act as if he were one of the guys. But he wasn't. He could hack out the chords, but he was not in the same league of any of the multitudes of young guitarists working in LA.

Still, the rehearsal went smoothly enough. Betts' musical repertoire consisted of standards, such as "I've Got Your Number" and "Witchcraft," mixed in with rock tunes like Michael McDonald's "I Keep Forgettin'" and America's "Woman Tonight." Skip was right. Betts could carry a tune. But like his guitar playing, his singing was marginal at best.

After less than an hour, Skip said, "Whaddya think, Chuck? We're ready."

Betts nodded. "Yeah, he's got it. Way better than that asshole Moo."

Skip grimaced slightly, then told the pianist, "Okay, then. Be at the Boiler Room on Sunset tonight and the next two nights. Gig's at eight. We'll be there by seven-thirty, latest. Know where it is?"

"Yeah. What's the wardrobe?"

"Black."

"Right."

Returning to the union's parking lot, his heart sank. The tire he had filled with fix-a-flat was once again flat. Apparently, the damage to the tire was too extensive. He had no choice but to change the tire in the parking lot. The Santa Ana winds baked him as he changed the tire, leaving him soaked with sweat.

With the tire changed, he drove up Vine Street to his favorite dry cleaners and told the owners, a gray-haired Korean couple, he needed two items just pressed, not cleaned – his black shirt and black pants. They were among the three staples of his musician's wardrobe.

First was his tuxedo, the full set, black tails and pants with the swirled seam. White shirt with the stiff collar, along with the black tie, cummerbund, and patent leather shoes. Next was his black suit, along with the white shirt, red tie, and black dress shoes –perfect for gigs such as wedding receptions and awards banquets. And finally, the black shirt, a short-sleeved collarless shirt that could be worn in orchestra pits or on smaller gigs, the ones that require musicians to be inconspicuous. The black shirt was paired with the black suit's pants and shoes.

He kept all of them in a garment bag which he stowed either in his storage locker or behind the Ford's seat. They stayed clean in the bag, but the tight quarters often left them wrinkled. The Korean couple took care of many musicians, and always turned in a first-class press job within an hour.

After dropping off the dry cleaning, he headed back out onto the westbound 101 toward the Valley. A short time later, he turned off onto the exit, drove beneath the freeway, and parked the Ford in the strip mall parking lot, next to a pet food store, a hair salon, and an insurance office. He looked further up the street and spotted a Denny's restaurant and a laundromat.

Both of those could come in handy.

He walked across the street to the church parking lot, and over to the chain link fence The fence was almost six feet tall, with shrubs and other landscaping blocking the view of the "bald spot." He followed the fence to its end point, about halfway between the street and the church, where it intersected with the hillside. He looked around, saw no cars in the lot, and climbed over the fence. Reversing course, he pushed his way through the weeds and up a small hill. After a few more feet, he found the open space. And he found the cause.

Someone had dumped about seventy cinder blocks on the ground, no doubt leftovers from the original sound wall project. They rested in a flat space between the trees and bushes. The bushes appeared to have grown around the dumped blocks. The open space felt slightly cooler, as the bushes and the high tree branches blocked the sun and the Santa Ana winds.

He walked through the open space, trying to avoid tripping over the scattered cinderblocks. He guessed the open space was about fifteen feet long and ten feet wide.

Big enough for a small-to-medium tent, that was for certain. Along with the cinder blocks, he noticed a large car tire, several soda pop cans, and some dirty flannel shirts.

Unbelievable, he thought. *The things people throw away. Not just throwing away, but dumping on the sides of roads and highways. Cinder blocks, and the lumber you saw getting dumped this morning …*

Despite the heat, he froze. *The lumber! And the cinder blocks! That's it!*

Okay, the lumber's an idea. But how are you going to get it in here without being noticed? The church folks might notice someone hauling lumber through their parking lot. Too say nothing of the cars passing by.

He walked farther forward, toward the gore point, until he found the gate. It was locked, but only by a small chain carelessly looped around the gate and through a lock.

Not much of a chain. But that makes sense. No one knows about the open space. No need for a pricey heavy-duty chain to keep people out.

Cut the chain, then haul the lumber through the gate. At night. It's a gamble, but it could work if you try to look official. Wear an orange vest, and gloves, and safety glasses.

Are you sure you can do this? Can't you just hear Dad saying, "You're better at piano than carpentry" yet again? Besides, you're running a risk of getting busted for trespassing on government property. Even a misdemeanor offense could hurt your chances of getting work. Hell, you got the gig with Betts. Any luck, you'll make enough to get either an apartment or a room.

Maybe. The gig with Betts might pan out, it might not. Until we know for sure, let's at least follow up on the lumber.

He drove back to the 405 exit where he saw the lumber-dumping take place. His heart sank when he saw a Caltrans maintenance crew loading the lumber aboard a massive orange Chevy stakebed truck. He decided to take a chance. He parked the Ford on the street and walked over to the work crew.

"Afternoon, men," he greeted them. "Looks like you got a load today."

The supervisor, a short, gray-haired man wearing a white hard hat and an orange vest answered, "Sure do. Someone dumped about a ton of lumber down the sides."

The pianist offered a sympathetic sigh.

"Damn, haven't these people heard of landfills?"

The supervisor laughed and said, "They've heard of them. And they've heard they cost money. Dumping doesn't."

The pianist offered another sympathetic sigh.

"I don't even want to ask what sort of stuff you guys have had to pick up."

This drew another laugh from the crew supervisor.

"We've had our share of exotic items."

The pianist decided it was time to gamble a bit. He said, "Listen, I was actually on my way to the lumber yard when I saw you guys. Any chance I can take some of this off your hands? It would save me some bucks. If nothing else, the taxpayers won't have to pay the landfill fees."

The supervisor hesitated.

"We can't load it into your vehicle. We have rules against assisting a private party."

"You won't have to. Just leave it on the ground out here."

One of the younger maintenance workers said, "Hey, Herman? What if I clumsily spilled some of the lumber we already loaded into the truck?"

Herman the supervisor glowered and said, "I'm going for a walk. Down to the 7-11 for a coke."

"I'll join you."

When the two had walked about fifteen feet, the pianist said, "Good idea. Don't think I want to witness that."

"Witness what?" Herman growled.

"Right. Listen, I'm also going to need some sheets of plywood. Know of any being dumped around here?"

Through a grim smile, Herman answered, "Other side of the freeway. We'll take care of that tomorrow. Same deal. Can you be here at nine?"

"I'll be here."

An hour later, his t-shirt and jeans again soaked with sweat, he finished loading the lumber into the little Ford's truck bed. It was a good haul of two-by-fours, varying in lengths of four, five, and six feet. The load filled the truck bed to about the halfway point.

He checked his watch. 2:20 p.m.

Let's head to the gym for a quick shower and a change of clothes. Then to the cleaners to pick up The Black, and onto the gig.

First, he had to secure his load. The Ford's truck bed was surrounded by chrome trim with snaps. The tarpaulin attached to the snaps. He opened the driver's side door, pulled the seat forward, removed the folded blue tarp, and spent the next several moments snapping the tarp into place over the load.

Okay, then. Good to go. Let's get cleaned up.

He drove toward Sunset and tried to avoid noticing one of the side streets. Seven months ago, he spent his first night sleeping in his Ford on that street.

He'd never thought it would come to that. He arrived in LA with some savings and an almost-new Toyota hatchback he bought during his senior year with the help of his mother's brother, Uncle Max. He started out in better shape than most, but soon discovered the brutal life of a new musician. The cost of living in LA ate up anyone's savings in a hurry. Established, experienced studio veterans with first-rate reputations made up the majority of working musicians. Gigs for the new guys came few and far between.

The pianist did all he could. He took low-paying, thankless gigs no established musician wanted. He always showed up on time or early. He tried his best to get along with the others, and never acted like some temperamental prima donna. He stayed completely clear of drugs, and only allowed himself an occasional alcoholic beverage.

He tried to save money by sharing apartments with roommates, but had a run of bad luck. Some roommates were undependable, others dishonest. A few were deeply troubled. He finally gave up and moved into a tiny studio apartment in Reseda. But even that proved to be too much. The sparse gigs just didn't bring in enough..

He made the tough decision to sell his Toyota. The cash from the Toyota could keep him going for another few months, perhaps just long enough for him to get some steady, better paying gigs. Until then, he'd need to find a cheap car to get around in. He found the Ford for a couple hundred bucks and sold the Toyota with great sadness.

It provided some cash, but it wasn't enough. Soon, he realized he could only make another couple of rent payments on the studio. He could face eviction, which would ruin his credit rating. Or he could put his belongings into storage and live in the Ford while he saved up enough for either a room or another studio apartment.

Trying to appear calm and dignified, he gave notice to his landlord.

"Where are you going?" the landlord asked.

"A new place in North Hollywood," he answered.

He spent several days moving his belongings into a storage locker in Van Nuys. With the apartment completely cleared out, he collected his security deposit check and drove to the union. After depositing the check, he spent several hours practicing, trying not to think about what had happened, and what was about to happen. As long as he played piano, he retained some feeling of self-worth. But soon, his joints started to ache, as if he had the flu. Again and again he told himself, *I am somebody. I'm not worthless. I'm not ...*

Just after five pm, he left the union, got a quick dinner of two AM-PM hot dogs, then drove aimlessly through Hollywood for several hours. Shortly before nine, he turned onto Sunset, then on to the side street. Covering the windshields and windows with the sun shades, he could barely bring himself to believe what was happening.

He was homeless. A vagrant, a bum. The onetime star of the Cincinnati Conservatory, whose senior recital was praised by the music editor of the Cincinnati Enquirer ... and it had somehow come to this. He was homeless and living in his car. He'd never known such humiliation. Thank God his mother didn't live to see this. And thank God his father didn't, either. His father would have never let him hear the end of it.

I am somebody. I'm not worthless.

He didn't sleep very well that first night. The humiliation made him sick to his stomach, so sick he almost threw up. Twice, he heard footsteps pass his car, and his body tensed with fear. He finally fell into a light doze for a few hours. When he woke, he had to remind himself where he was, and how he got there.

I'm going to get out of this, he vowed. *I'm not going to let it last that long. No matter what it takes, I'm going to get out of this.*

He never thought he would still be living in his Ford seven months later.

II

"Ladies and gentlemen, The Boiler Room is proud to present CHUCKIE BETTS!"

The pianist, Fred the bassist, and Skip the drummer played Rickey Lee Jones' "Chuck E's in Love Again" as Betts made his way from the rear of the darkened room onto the stage. The club appeared to be about three-quarter full of the one hundred-seat capacity, with the patrons gathered around tiny black circular tables.

Betts hopped on stage and launched into his routine. It consisted mostly of jokes about sex, and Hollywood celebrities, and life in LA. The pianist tried to listen, but his mind kept returning to the hidden open space, and the load of lumber stashed in the bed of his little Ford.

They swung into the first song, "Witchcraft." The Boiler Room's piano, a Yamaha baby grand, was in good shape. That was a relief. Plenty of clubs came with worn-out old pianos that required plenty of patience on the part of anyone playing them. The trio finished the last chorus of "Witchcraft," and Betts launched into another round of sex jokes.

Not many people are laughing. Can't blame them.

The gig ended at 10:00 pm. He saw Skip and Betts confer for a few moments. Then Skip walked over to the piano.

"Listen, you did all right tonight," Skip told him. "But one thing. Make sure you laugh at his jokes. Doesn't look good if we're sitting up here with stone faces."

"Sorry. First night for me. I was concentrating on doing the job."

Skip offered a sympathetic grin. "No sweat."

The pianist walked out into the warm evening air and retraced his steps down Sunset and up the side streets where he'd parked. As he turned a corner, he saw something that made his blood run cold – a Nissan with a smashed driver's side window and flashing emergency lights. On the sidewalk, a cop spoke with a crying young woman.

Poor girl. She looks nearly as shattered as her car window. Hope there aren't any other break-ins on this street!

He found the Ford where he parked it and let out a sigh of relief. No damage anywhere, not to the glass, not to the tires. The tarp that covered his load of lumber remained undisturbed.

He started the car, put it in gear, and headed toward a residential street in Hollywood where he'd parked before. The street was in a fairly good neighborhood. He always had to worry about two things – the raps on the windshield telling him to move on, and the risk of his car getting broken into, either when he was away, or when he was sleeping inside.

The risk of the latter, while not completely impossible, was pretty small. He drove what was quite possibly the most un-theftworthy vehicle in all of southern California.

Not long after he decided to sell his Toyota, he found an ad for a 1963 Ford Falcon Ranchero in the Pennysaver. The ad stated the car registered about 200,000 on the odometer and wasn't running. The asking price was four hundred dollars.

He drove to the Pomona address and found the Ford in the driveway of the owner, a dishwater blonde-haired middle-aged woman named Lori.

"Hello," he greeted her. "This the Ranchero in the Pennysaver?"

"That's the one. It was my father's. Interested?"

"Sure am."

He looked the Ford over. The Ranchero model was similar to a stock Falcon sedan, but with a pickup truck bed in place of the rear seat and trunk. Years of baking under the LA sun left the white paint chalky and faded. The blue plastic steering wheel looked even more chalky and faded. All the dashboard control knobs – snowy white when new – had yellowed with age. They resembled the teeth of a tobacco-chewing old man. The blue upholstery gave off a funky, grungy odor.

But his Ohio born-and-bred eyes saw one matchless advantage: A California vehicle, the Ranchero had no rust anywhere. Not on the body. Not on the frame. Not on the floorboards. His father always told him any car problem could be fixed – except rust and bent frames. The little Ford had seen better days, that was certain. But with no rust, it might as well have been brand new.

He popped the hood and took a moment to examine the oily, six-cylinder engine. He removed the air cleaner and examined the carburetor, and found it covered with a thin, dirty film. Lifting the distributor cap, he shined his key-ring flashlight into the distributor, and saw all the required parts—the rotor, points, and condenser.

They're probably worn out.

After replacing the cap, he told Lori, "Let's try to fire her up. Do you have any jumper cables?"

"No, I don't think so," she said.

He pulled a set of cables out of his Toyota and hooked them up, first to the Ford, then to Lori's Nova. He sat behind the Falcon's wheel. Lori started her Nova and let it run for a few moments. He turned the Ford's key. The starter *wruh-wruh-wruhhed.* The engine almost caught a couple of times. It sounded like it wanted to run, it was trying very hard. But it couldn't. He was pretty sure why.

He exited the car and offered Lori one hundred dollars. The two bargained for a bit and settled on two-fifty. He drove his Toyota over to a nearby auto parts store, bought a spray can of carburetor cleaner, and a new rotor, condenser, cap, and points. And a new battery.

An hour later, after cleaning the inside and outside of the carburetor with the carb cleaner, replacing the worn distributor parts, and installing the new battery, he turned the key again. The engine fired up, but it still didn't sound or feel quite right. In particular, the engine's idling was very rough. He had to hold the gas pedal down to keep the engine running. Once again, he knew why. He checked the exhaust and found some black smoke, the sign of too much unburned gas. But no white smoke. That was good. No burning oil.

Lori told him, "One other thing. Dad kept a blue tarp that covers the truck bed. It's yours of you want it."

"Sure do," he replied. "Thanks for everything."

He took the mildewed, funky-smelling blue tarp and stashed it behind the driver's seat. Then he limped the little Ford over to a gas station/garage. A mechanic produced a timing light and adjusted the distributor and point gap. Then the engine ran smoothly. For good measure, he had the mechanic change the engine and transmission oils.

He soon found the little Ford came with several ironic advantages. A thirty-year old half pickup/half sedan hybrid was not a prime target for car thieves. Its age and total lack of sexiness offered a certain amount of anti-theft security. The manual transmission offered another deterrent. Most car thieves had no clue how to work a manual gearshift. The Ford didn't even have the macho appeal of a Steve McQueen-style stick shift. Its gearshift came mounted on the steering column, the derisively-nicknamed "three on the tree," tipped with yet another yellowed knob. The six-cylinder engine provided indolent acceleration, which was just as well, as the old-style drum brakes required plenty of foot pressure.

The radio was the finishing touch. When he bought the car, he discovered the old AM radio didn't work. Rather than fixing it, he just removed it for repair at some later date when the extra disposable income might be available. The gap in the dashboard always reminded him of Edvard Munch's "Scream" painting. The absence of a radio provided thieves with even less motivation to break in. No self-respecting car thief would give the Ford so much as a passing glance. In a Zen-like way, the car's weaknesses were its strengths.

On the other hand, he knew he had to at least maintain a respectable appearance. When parking in a neighborhood not one's own, care must be taken to not draw attention to your car. If he let the Ford look like a complete beater, a junkyard refugee, the neighbors would know right away he was not one of them.

The day after buying it, he drove the Ford to a coin-operated car wash. After giving the car a thorough wash, he parked it next to a cinderblock wall. He removed the seat and the seat backs, and the tarp, and set them against the wall and let the hot southern California sun dry them out. For good measure, he sprinkled a box of baking soda into the insides of the seats, and a bit more onto the carpets. Then he spent more than four hours applying paint rejuvenator and several coats of wax to the body. He rubbed and rubbed until his hands and shoulders screamed in protest. When he finished, the Ford looked exactly as he hoped – like something belonging to an eccentric collector, an old but clean car awaiting total restoration, a restoration project that would get underway … oh, gee, any day now, really.

At first, he felt embarrassed when he pulled the car into a parking space at the union, or at a gig, or even at the grocery store. He learned the truth of the stereotype – people are judged by their cars, and nowhere more so than in southern California. The amused or pitying looks from those who watched him drive an unglamorous thirty-year-old relic stung him badly.

He also felt more than a bit of resentment. Circumstances had forced him to sell the Toyota, a car that he had purchased in Cincinnati with the help of his Uncle Max. He loved the Toyota, and gave it up only under great duress. The Ford was a poor substitute.

Yet in time, he started to warm to the little pickup. Both were in the same situation. At the very least, they were unappreciated. At worst, they were unwanted and unloved. The plain-looking Ford took him where he needed to go with no fuss or drama. It provided shelter. They were in this together. The car had earned his respect, and he did his best to take care of it.

He followed his usual morning routine of working out and showering at the gym. He finished by 8:00 a.m. and drove back to the same interchange on the San Diego Freeway where he'd collected the lumber. Only this time, he steered his car into a parking lot adjacent to the cross street. As promised, the orange Caltrans truck was parked on the curb. The men in the white hard hats and orange vests swarmed around the dark green bushes beneath the freeway, just past an open gate.

The pianist looked for and found Herman, the supervisor from the day before.

"Morning!" he shouted over the rumble of overhead freeway traffic.

"Morning. Here to pick up your load?"

"I'm ready."

"One thing," Herman told him. "The wood isn't plywood. It's sheets of OSB. Flakeboard. Do you have any gloves?"

"No, sure don't."

Herman shook his head.

"You'll need gloves to handle flakeboard. Rough stuff. There's a hardware store down the street. Get yourself a pair and we'll get to work."

"Will do. Will I also need a hardhat and vest?"

Herman nodded and said, "Wouldn't hurt."

The pianist got back in his Ford and found the hardware store about three miles down the side street. He bought a pair of gloves, then asked the checkout clerk, "Long shot, but do you have hard hats and vests?"

"Vests, yes. Hard hats, no."

The pianist bought the orange vest along with the gloves. He also picked up a pair of clear safety glasses, similar to the ones worn by Herman's crew.

Returning to the freeway, he found five sheets of the rough flakeboard piled on the sidewalk. The boards were painted brown and covered with ugly graffiti.

"Thing is," Herman said, as he loaned him a white hard hat, "These are four-by-eight. Your truck bed is only six feet long. You'll have to find some way to secure them."

The pianist placed the hard hat on his head.

"I can snap the tarp around the sheets and pick up some bungees from the hardware store. The lumber should stay in place."

Herman looked surprised.

"You haven't unloaded the lumber yet?"

Dammit! Should have thought of that!

"I had something come up last night," he told him. "Didn't get the chance."

"Okay. Help yourself to some flakeboard."

A half hour later, after shaking hands with Herman and the crew, he drove back to the hardware store. Once inside, he bought a set of bungee cords, a heavy-duty lock, a three-foot length of heavy chain, a plastic ruler-protractor, and a spiral notebook with unlined paper. Standing in the checkout line, he found his hands shaking.

Sure you want to do this? You're looking to break several laws. Trespassing, building without a permit, and God knows how many others. You're not the criminal type. Are you really sure about this?

Yes. I'm sure.

He drove to the Musician's Union, found a parking space and backed the Ford in, the better to avoid damage to either the wood sheets or another vehicle. Once inside the lobby, he checked the message board, chatted with several friends and associates, then crossed Vine Street to Vito's, an Italian restaurant much favored by musicians for both its food and proximity. Settling into a booth, he ordered an iced tea, pulled out the notebook, ruler, and a pencil, and got to work.

He'd noticed the bushes covered the open space at an irregular 45-degree angle, and decided a wedge-shaped structure would work best. Sort of an enclosed lean-to, or half of an A-frame. He figured a seven-foot tall structure would accommodate his five-foot eleven height. And it should be about nine feet long and five feet wide He used the ruler to draw the wall and floor. The slanting roof measured eight and a half feet from top to bottom.

That's a problem. Your longest pieces of lumber are just six feet.

That's okay. I can put splices on either side of the beams, and underneath them.

He drew the frames, consisting of three triangles, one at each end, the other in the middle.

How do you plan to build it? Won't be able to use a hammer or a saw. The noise will give you away in a heartbeat.

Glue and screws. No noise, and less chance of damaging the hands. I'll need to find a carpentry shop to do the sawing, and to pre-drill the screw holes.

Okay, then. But what sort of foundation are you looking at? Can't just set the thing on the ground.

That's what the cinderblocks are for. Dig six holes — one for each corner, plus two in the middle — each four feet deep. Pile the cinderblocks on top of each other, then bury them up to the four-inch mark. Stabilize the blocks with PVC pipes and sand.

How do you plan to attach the frame to the blocks? Anchor sleeves or masonry screws?

Go with masonry screws. They're cheaper, and will do the job —

The pianist shook his head and sighed.

Flakeboard. PVC pipes. Cinderblocks. Anchor sleeves and masonry screws. I'm starting to sound just like Dad. He'd be horrified. I know I sure as hell am.

He worked on the drawings for another two hours, then left the restaurant and crossed Vine back to the Union. After hunting up a copy of the Yellow Pages, he found a carpentry shop in Van Nuys, pulled out his phone and called the number. After sketching out what he had in mind, he heard a baritone voice say, "We can do it, but not until Monday."

"That's okay," he said "Thing is, could I drop the lumber and flakeboard off today? It takes up a lot of room, and my garage isn't that big."

"That's fine," the baritone replied. "Just drop it off before five."

He checked his watch. Just after one p.m. He had several hours before the carpentry shop closed.

Probably should get some practicing in.

The union building had several studios, and the bosses kept the hourly rental rates as low as possible. Even with the low rates, he tried to avoid practicing at the union, opting instead to practice on his Yamaha out at the storage yard. But even a high-quality electric piano like his Yamaha didn't have the proper feel of an acoustic piano. He knew he had to practice on an acoustic at least two or three times a week.

He started with the major keys: C, G, D, and on through the circle of fifths. Once through at a moderate, warmup tempo, then once again at a breakneck speed. Then once through the minor scales. Then the modes: Ionian, Dorian, Phrygian, Lydian, Mixolydian, Aeolian, and Locrian. Then through all the exercises of the Hanon book, which he knew without the book handy. He'd memorized them all a long time ago.

With the Hanon finished, he thought for a moment, and remembered one of his favorites. Ravel's "Sonatine." A delicate, complex, challenging piece. He placed his hands on the keyboard, played the first movement, was pleased to find he still remembered every note. Not just every note, but every nuance of every note.

He played it superbly well, but knew he still – after all these years – could not play it the way Audrey had. She brought something to that piece – and many others – that went well beyond mere technique. Audrey brought the soul of a poet to her playing.

That Audrey. She could have been something. Wonder what she would think about all this – living in the Ford and building the shelter. Pretty good bet she wouldn't think less of you for it. She'd understand.

He checked his watch. 1:35 a.m.

He'd been sitting in the Denny's, just up the street from the church parking lot, since 12:25. The gig with Betts had gone well. He remembered to laugh at the jokes, although it took no little amount of effort on his part. Once inside the Denny's, he ordered a bowl of chili, an ice water, and a decaf coffee. He slowly ate the chili while reading the LA Times. Despite the decaf, his pulse hammered. Earlier, he had dropped off the lumber and flakeboard that had to be sawn or drilled at the carpentry shop. The rest of the lumber could be used as-is, and was stored in the bed of the Ford.

This will be either the smartest thing you've ever done, or the dumbest.

At 1:50 he paid his check and walked out into the parking lot. He fired up the Ford and drove down the street to the point where the street and the on ramp intersected. Across the street, he saw the insurance office, pet food store, and hair salon. All were dark.

He shut off the ignition, reached under the seat, pulled up his toolbox and fished out a pair of heavy-duty shears. He climbed out of the car and walked to a dark spot between the streetlights. His pulse raced in the still-warm night air. Several cars roared above on the freeway, but he saw none on either the ramps or the street.

Here goes!

Dashing over to the gate, he cut the chain with the shears and pulled the chain clear. The gate swung open with a disconcertingly loud creak.

NOW!

He ran back to the Ford, unsnapped the tarp, pulled on his gloves, and lifted the first of the leftover lumber out of the bed. After another check for traffic, he ran through the gate with the wood in his hands and dropped it just behind the bushes. The grass and the bushes gave off a redolent, wilderness-like smell that felt, to him, like a warning of disapproval.

Despite the wild smell, he repeated the process, bringing two more armfuls of the lumber through the gate and dropping the pieces just behind the bushes. Next, he carefully walked through the dark to the open space, using his key-ring flashlight to guide him. He picked up two of the cinderblocks, hauled them back out to the Ford, deposited them in the bed and repeated that process two more times. Then he closed the gate, looped the new heavy-duty chain around the posts and closed the new lock through two links.

After one last check for traffic on the street and the on ramp, he drove the Ford back to the Denny's lot, pulled the tarp over the truck bed and secured it with the snaps.

Right. Let's go find a place to park for the night.

His watch beeped him awake at 5:30 a.m.

Damn! Just three hours sleep. Maybe I can sleep in for a bit …

No, you can't. Sleep later. Let's get the cinderblocks to the carpentry shop.

He drove up the San Diego Freeway to Van Nuys and took the exit for the carpentry shop. About a mile before the shop, he noticed a good-sized dumpster with a large piece of lumber sticking out.

Let's check this out.

He parked the Ford and walked to the gray steel dumpster. It stood just off the curb next to a half-demolished motel. Inside, he found several pieces of lumber. One was a three-by-three, about six feet long and with ragged edges, and another three-by-three, maybe five feet long. Also, three sheets of plywood, about three by five feet, and various pieces of drywall and other detritus.

Fantastic! The three-by-threes can be used as corner bracing blocks at each end of the frames. They'll work better than the lumber, which was the original plan. The plywood will make better gussets than the flakeboard.

Beneath the drywall pieces, he saw what looked like a curved piece of green plastic. He reached in, pulled it loose, and found it was a construction worker's hard hat. A crack ran along the top of the hat.

This is perfect! You already have the orange vest. Paint the hard hat white, and maybe you'll fool everyone into thinking you're a Caltrans worker!

He placed the hard hat on the front seat of the Ford, then tossed the three-by-threes and the plywood into the bed.

A few moments later, he pulled into the carpentry shop's parking lot. The sign read "Open 8:00 AM – 5:00 PM." He checked his watch.

5:50. Okay, then. You have a couple of hours. Let's grab some shut-eye.

"Thank you everyone! Good night!"

The trio kicked into another verse of "Chuck E's in Love Again" as Betts waded through the audience, occasionally high-fiving an audience member or two. A couple of times, he raised his hand, but got no response from the audience member.

Well, that's awkward!

The audience filtered out and the musicians began packing up. As usual, the pianist helped Skip pack up his drums. Betts came out from the backstage green room, took Skip aside for a few words, then left. Skip returned to the stage and approached the pianist.

"Hey, man, listen. Sorry, but Chuck just told me he wants another pianist."

"What? Why's that?"

"He says he can tell you were forcing the laughs."

Isn't he perceptive!

"Damn it," the pianist scowled. "This isn't going to help."

Skip patted his arm and handed him a check.

"Don't worry. Just about everyone knows Chuck is a total dickhead. No one'll blame you. I'll call you if I get something else."

"Thanks."

He stalked out of the Boiler Room, down Sunset, and up the side street to the Ford.

Dammit, this is so typical! So many musicians, a lot of them way better than me, must rely on marginally talented and marginally intelligent people for a paycheck. Why the hell can't smart people be in charge? The composer from Monday, Ed, was one of the few. Wish to God more were like him!

Settling into the Ford, he forced his foul mood aside. He drove north through Hollywood and then over to Burbank, and turned the Ford onto a side street, and then onto another, then parked. After placing the sun shades around the windows and windshield, he stretched out on the seat and hoped he could get a decent night's sleep without being hassled.

He awoke the next morning with a start. His watch was not beeping, as usual. He checked his watch. 7:20 a.m.

Shit! People will be up and about at this time! Must have slept through the alarm! Careful, now. Peek through the sun shades. Make sure no one is around.

He moved the passenger side window's shade slightly, and saw a gray-haired man sitting on his porch, drinking coffee. The old man hadn't noticed him. Yet.

Okay, make it quick! Haul it out of here before he notices!

He pulled the cardboard shades down and folded them, but didn't bother to stash them behind the seat. That could come later. He started the Ford, put it in gear, and quickly pulled out into the street. Out of the corner of his eye, he could see the old man watching him, but didn't have time to check the old man's expression, if any.

After about twenty feet he noticed a sheet of white paper held in place by the driver's side windshield wiper. At the first stop sign, he reached out and pulled the fluttering paper in. He opened it and was stunned by the words:

DO NOT PARK HERE AGAIN! WE KNOW YOU DON'T LIVE HERE! IF YOU PARK HERE AGAIN WE WILL CALL THE POLICE!

He slapped the steering wheel.

Damn it! Who the hell do they think they are? Is this a private street? Is it permit-parking only? Am I keeping them awake by blasting loud music? Hell, my truck doesn't even have a radio! What would the cops do to me? If they arrested all the homeless people in LA, they'd have to rent out both The Forum and The Arena to handle them all!

His mood deteriorated further as he drove to the gym. Even a vigorous, one-hour workout failed to stem his anger. He knew what he had to do. After a shower, he drove over to the self-storage yard, parked the Ford just inside the gate, and made his way to his locker.

He'd rented the small unit just before moving out of his apartment. It held his most important possessions — a metal strong box full of the important documents, some of his books, a suitcase, some tools, a bed frame, and his most important possession of all — a Yamaha electric piano.

Plenty of gigs required him to supply his own piano. He needed a secure place where it could be stored. The only drawback was the self-storage yard's hours — they closed at 8:00 p.m. and didn't reopen until 6:00 a.m. the following morning. On more than one occasion he had to stay awake after a late gig, driving around LA with the precious piano stored in the truck bed and surrounded by the custom-cut plywood sections that kept it from sliding around. He didn't dare let the piano out of his sight.

He removed the plywood sections, the piano stand and bench, then mounted the piano on the stand. He plugged the piano into a nearby wall outlet and ran through the entire Hanon book of exercises. They were like obstacle courses, scales with extra-space jumps, forcing the fingers to stretch and strike the keys accurately.

His fingers were as sharp and accurate as ever, and he allowed himself a smile of pride and satisfaction. Then he played, from memory, the first movement of Beethoven's "Pathetique" Sonata. The first movement started with the "Grave" section, very serious and dramatic. It quickly gave way to the Allegro di Molto e Con Brio section – equally dramatic, but fast, with much *brio*.

He played with plenty of brio, both hands starting in the lower register, playing what sounded like an ascending spiral, with harsh spikes at the top, then starting again. He spun the spirals and hammered the spikes. It felt good.

I can do this. I can play Beethoven and Ellington and just about any other type of music.

No more stupid dithering about whether to build the shelter. I'm going to build it. And I'm going to do everything I can to make sure I don't have to live there that long. Above all, I will never park on that street again. I will never set foot on that street again. Hell with them.

An hour later, he wheeled a shopping cart down the aisles of a hardware superstore, picking out the supplies he needed, carefully checking the prices.

Carpenter's glue. Plastic glue. Wood screws. Masonry screws. A shovel. A trowel. A small can of white spray paint. A mason's level. Twelve three-inch-wide PVC pipes, each four and a half feet in length. A ten-pound bag of sand. A good-sized gray canvas tote bag.

As usual, he felt ill at ease while shopping. He always had a lingering fear that someone would discover his secret and tell him, "No homeless allowed in here! Don't come back until you have a job and a place to live, like the other respectable people!" Even though he knew he had enough to pay for this day's shopping trip, the unease lingered.

He paid for his haul, then added some advertising fliers in the cart and wheeled it out to the parking lot.

Let's pull over to the corner and paint the hard hat right there.

He loaded up the Ford's bed with the PVC pipes, but kept everything else in the front seat, next to the hard hat. He drove over to the corner and pulled into a parking space.

After removing the liner from the hard hat, he spread the advertising fliers on the asphalt next to the passenger door, then set the hat on the fliers. Over the next few minutes, he sprayed the white paint over the inside and outside of the hard hat until all traces of the original green disappeared.

He looked back to see if any store employees were watching. They were notorious for not wanting any work done in their parking lots, which he supposed was understandable enough. God knows what sort of liability you'd face if someone hurt themselves on the premises. No one from the store watched him, but he noticed something he'd overlooked before – a McDonald's just next to the front entrance.

Why not? It's almost noon, and the paint is going to take a while to dry. We can afford to splurge a little.

He pulled the tarp over the bed and snapped it in place, then walked across the parking lot to the McDonald's, ordered a quarter pounder meal and took it back to the Ford.

The burger tasted good, a guilty pleasure. He tried to avoid spending his scarce dollars on too much fast food or junk food. More often than not, his money went to fresh fruits and vegetables, not processed junk. That part of his diet was a legacy of his time spent with Audrey, the strictest of strict vegetarians. God only knows what sort of chemicals and preservatives McDonald's used in the burger and the fries.

He thought of his first roommate when he arrived in LA. Danny, a fine sax player, seemed addicted to a steady diet of fast food and junk food. Only later did he learn Danny was addicted to a more sinister sort of junk. One night, he caught Danny trying to steal some money from his wallet. Danny denied it, again and again. It was no use. He told Danny he had to leave. Danny left.

It went downhill from there, from the unreliable or dishonest roommates, to the studio apartment, to living in the Ford. But he still kept an eye out for the "roommate wanted" postings on bulletin boards and in the LA Times. Even now. Potential roommates existed. Finding a good roommate would be infinitely preferable to his present situation.

The CHP could shut down this little project of yours at any minute. You get a promising lead on a roommate, or just a room, follow it up and don't think twice.

He finished the last of the french fries, drained his iced tea, and checked the hard hat.

The white paint was dry. After pouring some plastic glue over the inside crack, he set a small strip of plastic over the glue. He set the hat on the Ford's floor, and headed back to the bald spot.

Twenty minutes later, he parked the Ford in the strip mall lot and loaded his supplies into the canvas sack, except for the shovel. He replaced the liner in the hard hat, got out of the Ford, and donned the vest and hard hat.

Let's see what sort of bullshit artist I am.

Trying to look confident and businesslike, he walked down the sidewalk, sack in one hand and the shovel in the other. He unlocked and opened the gate. Without looking around – that would appear suspicious – he closed and locked the gate, then shoved through the bushes to the open space.

So far, so good. The wall and the fence hide just about everything, and what the wall doesn't hide, the bushes do. Still, his heart pounded.

The shade provided by the tree branches kept the open space a few degrees cooler. For that he was thankful, as the Santa Ana winds still gusted, and he had a lot of hard work ahead.

I can just see the real estate ads for this site: "Secluded, landscaped Valley location, easy freeway access ..."

His first task – clearing the bald spot of the cinderblock pile and other debris. The job took about thirty minutes. Even in the shade, the heat and the exertion left him sweating.

Water break?

No, not yet. Time enough for water and rest later.

The structure, as designed, was five feet wide and nine feet long. He chose a spot near the edge of the open space as the first corner. With his tape measure, he measured the other four corners and marked each corner with a cinderblock. Shovel in hand, he pressed down with his foot and started digging.

Four feet down at the northwest corner. Four feet down at the other corners. Two more holes at the halfway mark of the length. The dry soil felt soft but not overly thin or sandy.

The freeway traffic, although separated by the sound wall, hummed loudly, the noise occasionally punctuated by a jake-braking big rig. The Santa Ana winds still gusted. He wished they would ease up, and fretted they would blow hard enough to bend the tree branches and expose the open space to the surface road traffic.

Okay, now it's time to take a water break.

Just as he took his first swig from his canteen, he heard a police car siren coming from the direction of the Denny's and the strip mall. Despite the heat, he froze.

Don't make a sound!

The siren came closer, down the road, past the gate and under the freeway. It slowed for a moment ... then headed out onto the on ramp on the other side.

Whew! He took another swig of water to calm his pulse.

Fifteen minutes later, he sat cross-legged in the bald spot, marking each of the white plastic pipes with a sharpie. Each mark was six inches up from the bottom. The evening sun just started to set.

He picked up the first pipe, held it vertically, and squeezed it into the northwest hole up to the sharpie mark.

Try to imagine what the construction manual would look like.

Squeeze the second pipe into the ground just to the right of the first one.

Use the trowel to fill both pipes with sand.

Place the open holes of the cinder block over the pipes, and slide the block down to the bottom of the hole.

Fill the space between the cinder block holes and the pipes with more sand.

Okay! That's the beginning of the foundation.

He repeated the process at the other five locations, then called it a day due to darkness.

Not a bad day's work.

Yeah, but you're going to need some mortar between the cinderblocks.

No, I won't. The sand on the inside, and the soil on the outside, will hold everything in place. Besides, there's no way I could mix mortar on this site.

The sand and soil might handle the sideways loads. But what about the vertical loads? Shouldn't there be something in between the blocks? Some sort of gasket? This is earthquake country, after all. The blocks need something to absorb the shaking.

He stood and cast his eyes around the open space. After a moment he spotted something half-forgotten – the car tire, the one he'd tossed into the far corner with the other debris.

That's it! Cut up the tire into one-by-four-inch strips. Place them between each cinderblock, and between the cinderblocks and the wood structure. They'll absorb some of the shaking.

How do you propose cutting them up?

The carpentry shop has the saws. If they won't, I'll get a hacksaw.

The carpentry shop isn't open until Monday. That will set you behind one day. What will you do tomorrow?

He thought for several long moments.

So far, we've found the lumber, the flakeboard, the cinderblocks, and the tire all tossed onto the sides of the freeways. Tomorrow, let's make a check of every other off and on ramp and see what else we can find. When we're done with the 101 and the 405, we'll start with the 10. And if need be, we'll check out every other freeway in the Southland.

He awoke the next morning to the sound of his beeping watch, and was grateful that, this time, he heard it. He started the Ford and headed out from the residential Sherman Oaks neighborhood onto the Ventura Freeway.

Taking the first exit, he parked on the side street, donned his vest, hard hat and safety glasses, and walked over to the off ramp. Like most other ramps, it was surrounded by a chain-link fence. But at certain points, the fence was low enough to surmount.

He hopped over and found some cans and bottles, along with a few assorted fast food wrappers, but nothing useful. Overall, the ramp looked fairly clean. He guessed Herman and his crew had recently swept the place out.

Wouldn't want his job!

He crossed over to the on ramp, swung over the fence, and crunched his way through the weeds. Two mattresses lay side by side. He shuddered at the thought of the plant and animal life growing inside.

A rustling sound distracted him. He glanced to his left … and saw a good-sized rat gnawing on a half-eaten pizza.

Oh, shit!

He rapidly retraced his steps until he was back outside the fence.

Freeway rats! Great! Meet your new neighbors. What the hell am I doing here, anyway? I'm a graduate of the Cincinnati Conservatory. Why am I poking around all this junk and garbage?

Because I don't want to sleep in the Ford any longer. Keep going.

He returned to the Ford and drove down to the next interchange. After jumping over the on-ramp fence, he found paydirt –a bookcase made of walnut-veneer particle board. It looked to be about six feet tall and seven feet wide, with eight shelves and a fake-walnut cardboard backing.

Good! Better than good! Perfect! This is the floor! The beginning of one, anyway. The boards look to be about a half-inch thick. Any luck, we'll find some more dumped furniture like this.

Further up the ramp, deeper into the weeds, he found more in the way of cans, bottles, wrappers, clothes, cardboard boxes and tires. Nothing of use. He retraced his steps and crossed over to the off ramp. About halfway up, he spotted a piece of bright blue plastic.

He picked it up and discovered it was an old AM transistor radio, an Emerson, the kind not manufactured in years.

Not much use for these. Just the AM band. Besides, if it's been sitting here long enough it probably doesn't work.

On the other hand – AM is at least good for news and traffic reports. Especially the traffic reports. You lucked out the other day when the accident didn't keep you from the Betts rehearsal. What the hell — buy a battery and see what happens.

An hour later, the bookcase lay disassembled in the weeds of the on ramp. One by one, he raised the bookcase parts over the fence and down onto the grass next to the ramp shoulder. Then he retrieved his Ford, parked it on the shoulder, and loaded the bookcase components into the bed, in full view of everyone passing by. No one gave him a second glance. He was just a guy in a hard hat and vest, cleaning up freeway debris. The fact that this was a Sunday, not a workday, didn't seem to occur to anyone. Neither did anyone notice his little pickup was not a Caltrans truck.

You'd better hope no actual Caltrans workers pass by. They won't be so easily fooled. They'll know in a heartbeat you're not one of them.

He drove over to a drug store, filled his canteen from a water fountain, and bought a generic nine-volt transistor battery. Back in the Ford, he took several long swigs of the water. The Santa Anas still gusted, and the temps remained in the upper nineties. Beneath the orange vest, sweat soaked his white polo shirt.

After a few minutes, he gently pried open the rear housing of the radio and snapped the new battery into place. He replaced the housing, extended the telescoping antenna, and rolled the on-off/volume button clockwise. After a few seconds, he heard a lovely sound. The sound of … static.

Damn thing works!

He rolled the tuner button and heard the *op-op-op* of stations passing by, then settled on 1070. Female voices sang, "K-N-X Ten-Seventy, News Ray-Dee-Ohh …"

Whaddya know? Now I won't be totally blind while I drive around LA

That night, he decided he'd had such a good day, he would allow himself an almost unimaginable indulgence – a proper Sunday dinner, in the form of a chef's salad at the Denny's. He savored every bite of the ham, the hard-boiled eggs, the lettuce, the ranch dressing. And he reviewed his day's haul.

What a haul it was. At almost every interchange, he found something of value. A black, ten-by-twelve heavy duty truck tarpaulin, the perfect covering for the roof. A five-foot long oak veneer record cabinet, designed for LPs, made of half-inch particle board, just like the bookcase.

A small desk made of the same. That gave him just about enough particle board for the floor. Numerous pieces of packing styrofoam, which he could use for insulation. Several sheets of plywood, perhaps enough to finish covering the wall and sides.

He thought of the items he couldn't use. An appalling number of easy chairs, sofas, and mattresses, each one no doubt hosting interior "science projects" of varying degrees of grossness. More tires. Car batteries. Bicycles in various states of disassembly. Office supplies, binders, quarterly reports from 1989.

Shaking his head, he thought, *Hasn't anyone in LA ever heard of a city dump?*

III

After his usual Monday morning workout and shower, he drove over to the carpentry shop and dropped off the veneer particle boards, the plywood, and the tires. The man at the desk, a surprisingly slight young blonde man with the deep baritone phone voice, looked a bit puzzled, but said he could cut the tires into the strips that he wanted. The baritone also told him he'd have the rest of his order done later that day.

He stopped by the Hollywood post office and collected his mail, which consisted of a letter from his sister. Then he drove to a tire store on Vine Street and asked the young man in charge of the service desk if they could replace the driver's side front tire, the same tire damaged by the freeway debris one week ago. The young man checked and found they had the right tire in stock and could mount it in about an hour. The pianist signed the work order and handed the young man the keys to the Ford. Then he took a seat in the gray-tiled, tinted glass-windowed lobby, plugged his cell phone charger into a wall outlet and began reading the letter from his sister.

She was busy preparing for the new school year. One of her friends, a history teacher named Dave, had been promoted to Vice-Principal. The taxes on the house were due. The roof might be good for just one more winter.

He smiled at the irony. Quite possibly, he was the only homeless person who was also a homeowner. When his father died, he left the house to both daughter and son. Perhaps it was some small attempt by his father to appear even-handed. More than likely, his father thought his son would never make it in Hollywood and would need a place to live once he admitted defeat and came back home.

I'm not ready to admit defeat.

Besides, he knew his sister benefitted from the house. Her middle school biology teacher's salary went a lot farther without the massive bite of monthly rent or mortgage payments. She paid the property taxes and the upkeep on the house. He promised himself he would help out, someday, when he was able.

The ringing cell phone interrupted his musings. He let the phone ring twice — *never answer on the first ring!* — then flipped it open.

"Hello?"

"Hey big guy, it's Marty Morris. You worked as a rehearsal pianist for us last year, remember?"

"Sure do. Had a great time. What can I do for you?"

"Short notice, but I've got a new show in the works and need an audition pianist. Are you free Wednesday and Thursday this week?"

He forced himself to pause.

"Hmmm, let me check my calendar … yeah, as a matter of fact I'm free those days. Where and when?"

"Hartz Theater on Sunset. Nine AM."

"I'll be there."

"Thanks, man. See you there."

He closed the phone and gave a sigh of relief and satisfaction. Marty Morris ran a theater company in Hollywood, specializing in new works, both musical and non-musical. The job was harder than it sounded. Hollywood, the film and television capital of the world, could be an iffy place for live theater. Marty's usual practice was to hire at least one established film or TV star who wanted to keep up his or her theater chops. But even the presence of a star was no guarantee.

Still, this was good news. He'd worked for Marty as both audition and rehearsal pianist last year. At times, the rehearsal pianists were retained as orchestra conductors for the run of the show. A long-running gig like that could bring in some good steady money.

Maybe. One step at a time.

The cool night air felt colder every moment. Earlier in the day, the Santa Ana winds vanished almost in an instant, bringing both the ocean breezes and the smog back to the Southland. For once he wished the smog could be thicker, thick enough for him to hide in.

The guys at the carpentry shop had finished his project on time, even with the last-minute addition of the tire-slicing. With his Ford packed full of lumber and plywood, he headed back to the Denny's and waited until eleven thirty. When the time came, he drove down to the gore point, where the side road met the on-ramp, and where the locked gate awaited him.

He unlocked the gate, unsnapped the cover from the Ford's bed, removed it, and gathered a load of lumber in his left arm. He used the keychain flashlight in his right hand to guide him through the weeds and landscaping. All went well until his third trip. Just as he exited the gate, an iron voice commanded, "Hold it! What's going on?"

He looked to his right and saw a Highway Patrol cruiser parked in front of the Ford. The cruiser's headlights were on high beams. He could barely make out the face in the driver's seat.

"Good evening, Officer," he said, trying to keep the adrenaline out of his voice as he launched into his rehearsed script. "Sorry for the trouble. I work for a construction contractor. We have a deal with Caltrans to use this space for staging. My crew was supposed to bring in the equipment and supplies today. But they spaced on it. If I don't get all this shit in place by six AM, I'll have hell to pay."

The faceless officer stayed quiet for several moments, then said, "What's the lumber being used for?"

"Falsework," he answered.

The cop remained quiet for another couple of very long moments, then replied, "Looks like you got the short end of the stick."

"Yes sir, kind of."

"Okay, then. Good luck on the project."

"Thank you, sir. Have a good night."

The CHP car pulled away down the road, toward the on ramp.

Jesus Mary and Joseph!

His heart-pounding felt like the cannons from the 1812 Overture. Despite the cold, he sweated rivers. He wanted to sit down and catch his breath, but decided against it.

No, get back to work. Finish this up ASAP. Can't believe I actually got away with that. Maybe I should switch from piano to acting!

Twenty minutes later, he finished unloading the last of the "equipment and supplies."

Let's spend the night at LAX. I've had enough excitement for one day!

At six the next morning, he parked in the strip mall parking lot. He got out of the Ford, put on his hard hat, vest, and glasses, and walked down the road until he came to the fence. His heart pounded harder than expected. He unlocked the gate and entered. Without obviously looking around, he checked to see if anyone was watching. Seeing no one, he closed the gate behind him and clicked the lock shut. Pushing through the weeds and bushes to the open space, he found the lumber, plywood, flakeboard, and supplies where he'd left them the night before.

He picked up four tire-strips, placed them on the southeast-most cinderblock, slid another block down the plastic pipes, then repeated the process three more times. The fifth block protruded above the ground by about four inches, just as he'd wanted. He repeated the process at the other five locations. Once all the blocks were set, he shoveled soil around the sides. When he finished, he found himself thinking the six blocks looked more like a set of bridge piers than a normal house foundation.

After a celebratory swig of water, he got to work on the framing. He remembered the time in high school when he read Salinger's "Raise High the Roof Beams, Carpenters."

Before I can "raise high" the roof beams, I have to join them together.

The roof beams had to be eight and a half feet long, but none of the lumber pieces he'd found were long enough. The carpentry shop trimmed some of them into three six-foot segments and three two and a half-foot lengths. He used some shorter segments as splices, and glued and screwed them into place.

The sight of the lumber stacked in the sunlight brought an unexpected rush of painful memories. His stomach soured. Once again, he heard his father sneering, "Good thing you're better at piano than carpentry."

Yeah, I know, I'm not much of a carpenter. Any luck, I'll be just good enough to pull this off.

He tried to ignore both the unpleasant memories and the sound of passing traffic on the freeway, the ramps, and the street. At one point, the sound of another eighteen-wheeler jake-braking down the off ramp startled him. He was certain the big rig driver must have hit the jake-brake after seeing the roof beams. But after a shaky few moments, he made sure the bushes and walls still hid the open spot from passing traffic, and resumed work.

Within fifteen minutes, all three roof beams lay on the ground. He allowed himself another ten minutes to rest and drink water from his canteen. After making sure the glue was dry, he thought *Okay, then. Back to work. Once more, imagine what the construction manual would say.*

Join the roof beam to the side beam.

Join the floor beam to the others.

Insert the support beams into the frame.

Add the gussets.

He joined the pieces together, all the while pouring the glue and grinding the screws into the holes.

One frame down. Two to go. Might as well enjoy it. This is as much screwing as you'll be doing anytime soon!

Attach the first two floor cross beams.

Here we go. Let's put this all together. Raise High the Shed Frames, Not-Much-of-a-Carpenter!

He stood the first frame upright and used the mason's level to make sure the floor was straight. It tilted down to the south. He stuffed a piece of cardboard between the floor beam and the cinderblock foundation until the frame was level, then attached it to the cinderblock with the masonry screws.

Over the next hour, he joined the frames together with more cross beams, both at the bottom and the top, all of them connected by the corner blocks. The constant grinding-in of the screws left his hands swollen, sweaty, and sore.

When he finished, the three skeletal frames stood with pride, bound together as one unit, attached securely to the cinderblock piers, with the remaining tire strips acting as gaskets between the floor beams and cinderblock foundations.

I'll be damned! It's actually starting to look like something!

Yeah, it is. Exactly what, I don't know. A cheese wedge? A door stop?

Well, as a matter of fact … it looks a little bit like the musical symbol for a crescendo, a letter V stood on its side. A triumphant, confident increase in volume.

Or, looking at it another way, it could be the opposite. A diminuendo, a shrinking of volume. That's a more accurate description of life these days.

He thought for a long moment.

No. This little shanty is a crescendo. A big step up from living in the Ford. Call it The Crescendo House. Or better yet … this is California. Call it Casa del Crescendo. Okay, then. Casa del Crescendo it is. Now get back to work.

Over the next hour, he attached the flakeboard to the roof and the plywood to the sides, and surprised himself with how smoothly everything came together. The floor came next. That's when he ran into his first snag.

He slid a six-foot bookcase frame piece along the floor beam up to where the floor and the roof met, and realized he forgot something. All the particle board pieces had square edges. The roof angled at fifty-five degrees and just barely touched the top corner of the floorboards.

That won't work. Need a better seal than that. The floorboards need to be beveled.

No big deal. I can run the boards over to the carpentry shop.

Yeah, but can you imagine what Dad would have said about that?

He thought for several long moments.

No need to imagine. I know damn well what he'd have said.

He dropped the floorboards off to the blonde baritone at the carpentry shop, and headed over to the hardware superstore for some door hinges and latches. He tried not to think about his father, but the redolent smell of the carpentry shop's freshly cut lumber brought another rush of memories.

His father was one of the top men with the Cincinnati office of Anson, Pawling, and Associates, one of the country's biggest civil engineering firms. Like many engineers, his brilliance with advanced mathematics was mirrored by a lack of facility with words. Quick to grasp esoteric ideas and original thinking, he lacked the ability to express such thoughts either orally or in writing. At work, he relied on one of his junior engineers to write the all-important project reports. The junior engineers would never match the father's engineering brilliance, but they knew how to put the design concepts and construction techniques into something resembling coherence and clarity.

The father had no such help at home. When the pianist was eight, his father decided the two of them should work together on a tool shed to be built in their back yard. The father tried to explain the fundamentals of carpentry, but couldn't put the basics into words an eight-year-old could understand. On the second day, after watching his son struggle with the saws and hammers, he snapped, "Just watch the way I do it!"

The son watched. He tried to learn, but it took time for a young boy to acquire the basic skills. Years later, his piano teacher would tell him, "Before you become any good at anything, you're going to be bad for a long while. Both students and teachers have to grit their teeth through plenty of bad."

That was his father's other flaw, a lack of patience. He expected his son to learn every task quickly, and to perform them flawlessly on the first try. By the time the shed was finished, father and son barely spoke.

Still, his father insisted his son assist him on other projects, every one of which the son dreaded and struggled through. A new upstairs bathroom. A new front porch. The father's pride and joy, a '68 Pontiac GTO convertible.

Things came to a head four years later, when the father decreed that the house needed an addition. The new room would be a game room, something the entire family would enjoy.

Laying the foundation was bad enough, with his father haranguing him to make certain just the right amount of mortar was applied, and to see to it the cinderblocks were perfectly straight and aligned.

The framing was worse. His father chose a Saturday morning for the framing. The day dawned warm and humid and grew more hot and humid with every hour. He sawed four beams, all the while sweating in the humid sunshine and listening to his father's snarling critique. While sawing the fifth beam, the saw slipped in his sweaty hands. The teeth cut into the skin between his left thumb and forefinger. He dropped the saw, grabbed his hand and yelled. The pain caused him to yank his left hand up and down, left and right.

Then came the moment he never forgot. His father laughed, a belly laugh of great amusement at his son's clumsiness. Just then his mother came out to tell them their lunch was ready. The mother saw the son jumping around and yelling in pain. She saw the blood that was just starting to pour out of the sliced-open skin. And she saw the father laughing.

She ran to the father and slapped him, hard. He tensed and roared at her, "What the hell is your problem?"

"LOOK at him!" she shouted. "He's bleeding!"

His mother took him inside, wrapped the wound in an ice-filled towel, and drove him to the emergency room. The doctor sewed up the cut with three stiches and bandaged it. When they returned home, he hid in his room while his mother and father had it out. Even with his door closed, he heard them clearly.

"I didn't see the blood," his father insisted. "I didn't know it was that serious."

"It doesn't make any difference," his mother snarled. "Laughing at your son's pain was cruel. I can't respect any man who would laugh at someone else's pain, especially that of his own son."

Their marriage died that night. The two of them were cut apart just as violently as the skin between his thumb and forefinger. No amount of stitching could join them back together.

They didn't divorce. He often thought it would have been better if they had. They moved into separate bedrooms. They spoke to each other in tones of icy politeness. The father seemed to regard his wife as the hired help, someone he paid to run the house and raise the children, a sort of half-housekeeper, half-governess. She made it clear that he damn well needed her to do both.

The father spent as much time away as possible. At work, he volunteered for projects that took him out of Cincinnati, and sometimes out of the country, for months at a time.

When he returned, he spent his weekends aboard a large power cruiser he kept in a marina on the Ohio River. He threw plenty of weekend parties aboard the boat for his engineering buddies. No one ever explicitly said so, but everyone knew – plenty of women attended those parties. The mother never complained. She seemed more relieved than angry at the idea of the father giving his attention to other women.

The father finished the house addition by himself and bought a pool table as the centerpiece of the new game room. But by then he was absent most of the time, and the pool table remained unused. The real centerpiece of the room was the new Baldwin baby grand piano the mother bought just a few months after the sawing accident. (Fortunately, his hand healed without complications.) The game room, with its thick carpet and foam ceiling muffling the sound, became the pianist's de facto studio, where he could practice for hours on end without bothering either his mother or sister. Or, on the rare occasions when he was home, his father.

———————

Once inside the hardware store, he ran through his shopping list: Two cans of black spray paint. One can of varnish. Two paint brushes. Two door hinges. Latches that locked on both the inside and outside. One lock. One tube of caulking.

One the way back to Casa del Crescendo, he decided, on impulse, to stop into a drug store and buy something he'd seen several months ago — a single-use camera. The idea was that a person would use the camera to take 24 photos, then turn in the entire camera, rather than just the film. In a few days, the drug store would have the photos ready.

Why not? This is not the sort of project you see every day. Might as well make a record of it.

Three hours later, he called it a day and reviewed his progress. He'd fitted the tarpaulin over the roof and attached it with screws to the sides and the bottom of the overhang. About four feet of the tarp extended beyond the top of the roof. He decided to turn the excess into a porch of sorts, with the leftover lumber as supporting "columns." He spray-painted the tarp and the sides black and varnished the inside of the roof and walls. Then he finished installing the door frame and the door hinges, snapping photos of every step.

Almost done. Any luck, I'll be able to move in this weekend at the latest.

Okay, then. While we're at it, check out the new neighborhood. See if there's anything useful.

He retrieved the Ford from the Denny's parking lot and drove northward. He found very little of interest — a gas station and a 7-Eleven. After a few blocks the street dead-ended. A public park lay in the path.

Reversing course, he drove south, past the interchange and past the Denny's strip mall. Barely a block later he found a small commercial center that contained, among other things, a self-storage business.

Interesting.

He parked and walked up to the office. Inside, he found a tired-looking gray-haired woman at the desk.

"Help you?" she asked limply.

"Yes, I'm interested in a unit," he said, summoning all his dignity. "Do you have a price list?"

The woman handed him a brochure without comment.

Scanning the brochure, he saw that the same-sized unit he rented in Van Nuys was more expensive. Better yet, a larger unit – four feet by six feet – cost only a few dollars more per month.

"What are your hours?" he asked.

"24-7."

Even better! The Van Nuys place closes at eight pm.

"May I see one of the four-by-six units?" he asked.

The woman led him out of the office and into a dark hallway. Metal doors lined both sides of the hall. She produced a key and opened one of the doors.

He looked inside and thought, *Perfect! I could use it as a studio, and practice for hours without bothering anyone. Or without anyone bothering me.*

They returned to the office, and he spent the next several minutes filling out the numerous forms. Soon, he was all set. He'd move his stuff in on the first of the month.

He found a surprising spring in his step as he walked back to the Ford.

I'm moving up in the world, he thought. *First, my living accommodations. Now the storage unit. Tomorrow, the world …*

He pulled out of the parking lot and headed south again. The boulevard was lined with a couple of car dealerships, one Italian and one Chinese restaurant, small office buildings, a bicycle shop, and other commercial establishments. All in all, it seemed a typical San Fernando Valley landscape. But he was pleased to see so many parking lots. He could alternate parking the Ford in different lots from night to night. No more worries about attracting attention by parking in the same place every night.

Fact is … why not think about sleeping in the storage unit? More room, and it's climate controlled. It's not built illegally next to a freeway.

No, that's no good. They have security cameras, and probably plenty of experience with people trying to save money by sleeping in the units. You'll get tossed out on your can if you're caught. Besides, the doors don't lock from inside.

Worth thinking about, though. The CHP or Caltrans can shut down the shed at any minute.

Just a few moments earlier, he had felt almost buoyant. Now, the depressing realities once again pressed in on him. His life was reduced to three options – sleeping in an illegal wooden shed, or surreptitiously sleeping in a storage unit, or once again sleeping in his Ford.

Things have got to get better. Soon.

———————————

"If he walked into my life …"

A young black woman with curly brown hair and almost-Asian eyes sang the song with great feeling in her alto voice. He accompanied her, listening for the nuances in her voice and matching those nuances on the piano keys. She appeared to be just under thirty. A sleeveless one-piece red dress displayed her voluptuous figure to good effect.

The two of them finished the song with an extended chord. Silence followed for a few moments. Then a bored-sounding middle-aged woman's voice in the front row said, "Thank you. Be sure the desk has a copy of your head shot."

The young singer exited stage left. The pianist checked his watch.
1:45 PM.

For the past day and a half, he'd accompanied prospective cast members of Marty Morris' new musical. At times, he felt as if he were accompanying every singer/actor in Los Angeles. Some of them were superbly talented, and he wondered why they were not more successful. Some were equally good, but seemed too aware of it, and carried an air of haughtiness. Others were not so good but every bit as arrogant. Some of the best, like the young black woman, came across as completely un-self-conscious. Most were young. He guessed they had probably arrived in Los Angeles about the same time he'd shown up. He wondered how many of them slept in their cars. Probably more than a few.

But several were older, in their mid to late forties or even their early fifties. They'd been in the business for a quarter century or more, yet were still auditioning for roles, still enduring rejection after rejection, still hoping to snag that one role that would take them to the top, still unwilling to admit defeat. They made for a sad sight, and the pianist heard overtones of deep aching in their voices.

That won't be me. No way I'll hang around to the point where I'm an object of pity. If I don't make it, I'll clear out of town and won't even leave a forwarding address.

He deposited his check in the Union ATM, scanned the bulletin boards, and spotted his friend Skip the drummer in the lobby.

"Hey, Skip, what's up?"

"The usual no good," Skip answered with a grin. "How about you?"

"The same. Just came from a gig. Audition pianist. You still working with Chuckie?"

Skip's face twisted into a sour grimace.

"Nah. The Boiler Room didn't renew him. Wasn't drawing any crowds. He's working just one night a week at another club, and accompanying himself. Can't afford a trio anymore."

"Couldn't happen to a nicer guy," the pianist replied. He and Skip shared a bitter laugh.

The two of them chatted for a few more moments. Then he left the union and drove to the Van Nuys carpentry shop. His hands almost tingled with anticipation. He paid the blond baritone, tossed the boards into the back of the Ford, and headed up Vine Street.

Almost done! Why not stop by the Vons on Sunset and pick up some cheap wine? Maybe even some fried chicken. Let's celebrate a little.

He pulled into the Vons parking lot and covered the Ford's bed.

Not that the boards are worth much, but you never know — some people steal just for the kicks of it.

Once inside, he found a four-pack of small bottles of Chardonnay and some plastic glasses. After ordering a fried chicken breast and drumstick, he headed back to Casa del Crescendo.

An hour later, he finished the floor. The beveled ex-bookcase boards slipped neatly between the roof and floor beams. The rest of the floorboards slid into place with no trouble. Beneath the boards, he'd glued more styrofoam packing for insulation. He screwed the last of the plywood to the frame, attached the door to the door frame, and hooked up the door latch. Then he stood back and looked everything over.

Structurally, she's done. Still some more work to do — painting, varnishing, caulking, attaching the cardboard bookcase backing to the wall — but the basic structure is done, all according to plan.

He took a few more photos, then stepped inside, opened the first small bottle of Chardonnay, and poured it into a plastic glass.

Here's to Casa del Crescendo! She may not look like much, but she's home. For now.

He took a sip of the wine, then stopped. He cocked his ear.

Plop! Plop! Plop!

He stood still and listened.

Sounds like … rain. Well, that's right, KNX said there would be a chance of light sprinkles tonight.

At that moment, the light plopping sounds turned into a steady drumroll. He leaned his head outside the door and watched as the rain fell in heavy drops. Soon, the rain soaked the ground into a muddy mess. He smelled the rain and the soil and the wet bushes. But the inside of the shed remained dry.

He finished the chicken and the glass of wine, and allowed himself the reward of a second glass of cheap Chardonnay. He knew his accomplishment was rather modest. He'd built — illegally — a wedge-shaped shed, and it didn't leak during a rain shower. Nothing to crow about. But victories and triumphs had been few and far between this year. Modest or not, his project was a success. So far.

Any luck, it will lead to others. I'll spend one more night in the Ford.

The next day, he finished the last of the painting, varnishing, and caulking just after two p.m. All would take several hours to dry out.

Okay, then. Off to the camping supply store.

From the moment he started building Casa del Crescendo, he knew he would need some camping equipment once the shed was finished. He'd spotted the Van Nuys store a few weeks ago, just off the I-405 Victory Boulevard exit, and had filed away the location for future reference.

Just after exiting the Victory Boulevard ramp, he spotted a sign that read, "Yard Sale."

Beneath the words, an arrow pointed to the left. He decided to check out the sale. He followed more signs – one right turn, and two more left turns – until he came to a split-level home with various household items cluttering the otherwise immaculate green lawn.

Two items caught his attention right away – a sleeping bag with a liner, and an air mattress. Next to it he found a small blue vinyl pup tent.

The tent's too small. But the sleeping bag, liner, and air mattress are just what I'm looking for.

He explored further and found a one-burner camping stove, a can of stove fuel, and a two-by-three-foot insulated cooler. Also, a classic Boy Scout mess kit – aluminum pots and pans of various sizes, with a detachable handle that fit them all. A battery-powered lamp and a water jug rounded out the treasure trove.

This is everything I need!

"Good morning," a voice from behind him said.

He turned and found a six-foot, gray-haired man with deep furrows in his forehead.

"Good morning."

"You look like you're interested in the camping gear," the gray-haired man said. "Do much camping?"

"A bit," the pianist replied. "This equipment brings back some memories. That stove, the classic Coleman 400. And the mess kit. I used both when I was in the Scouts."

"They belonged to my grandson," the man replied. "Eagle Scout."

"I made Star Scout. Had a good time and learned a lot. I guess your grandson just lost interest in camping?"

"No," the man replied. "He passed away. Cancer. Six months ago."

"Oh. I'm sorry."

"Thank you. Are you interested in any of this?"

"I'm interested in all of it. Let me hit an ATM, and I'll be right back."

A half-hour later, he loaded all the equipment into the Ford. Shaking hands with the gray-haired man, he said, "Thanks for everything."

"Thank you."

"I'll … I promise to take good care of your grandson's gear. Scout's honor."

The man offered a sad smile. "Appreciate that."

He headed back to Casa del Crescendo, all while shaking his head in amazement at his great fortune. One single yard sale provided him with everything he needed at a fraction of the cost of new. He even bought the tent. Small as it was, he could still use it for storage. He didn't want to keep the stove or the can of stove fuel inside the shed, not with all those fumes. But he didn't want to store them out in the open, either. The small tent was perfect.

He also felt sorrow for the misfortune that made all the equipment available. The look of quiet suffering in the old man's face haunted him.

I can't imagine the pain of burying your own grandchild.

Moments later, the gray skies opened. Massive raindrops battered the Ford.

I'm going to need an umbrella.

He pulled into a Sherman Oaks shopping center and found a Vons grocery store and a drug store. Inside the drug store, he hunted down a black umbrella and batteries for the camping lamp. At the Vons, he found ice for the cooler and water jug, hot dogs, a box of resealable plastic bags, a roll of paper towels, and more fried chicken.

I'll have the chicken tonight. If it stops raining tomorrow, we'll break in the stove with the hot dogs.

Twenty minutes later, he parked the Ford on the shoulder next to the gate leading to Casa del Crescendo. The rain pounded harder.

Keep that rain coming! This way, no one will pay any attention to anything I'm doing.

He donned his hard hat, vest, and glasses. After covering himself with the umbrella and unlocking the gate, he brought the stove and the can of stove fuel up to the front door. He set both down beneath the overhanging tarp, and made several trips back to the Ford, bringing the rest of the gear back into the shed. After parking the Ford up the street, he walked, umbrella in hand, back to Casa del Crescendo. His sneakers glopped through the muddy ground, and the wet weeds left his jeans cold and damp. The moment he stepped inside the shed, the rain fell with full fury.

Not a moment too soon!

He removed his muddy shoes and left them by the doorway. After dropping the bag of ice into the cooler, he placed both the hot dogs and the last two small bottles of Chardonnay on top of the ice bag. The rain pounded like several sets of tympani mallets on the roof. The shed's interior gave off the sweet, happy smell of fresh varnish.

He removed the lamp cover and snapped the new batteries into the sockets. After replacing the cover, he moved the switch to the ON position and was rewarded with the soft glow of the lamp. The cheerful light gave the interior of Casa del Crescendo a warm, nearly homey ambience, almost in defiance of the pounding rain.

He closed the door, unrolled the air mattress and spent several moments blowing into the air stem until the mattress was inflated. After unrolling the sleeping bag, he stuffed the liner inside, then placed the sleeping bag on top of the air mattress. He took a moment to look things over.

I guess this isn't too bad, for the time being. Looks like I might get a better night's sleep on this setup than I've been getting in the Ford. At least I can stretch my legs all the way out. I'll take any improvement I can get.

He retrieved the small wine bottle from the cooler and poured the contents into the plastic cup. Once again, the Chardonnay and the fried chicken tasted like the height of luxury. After finishing the wine and the chicken, he chastised himself for not buying plastic trash bags. That would be the first order of business tomorrow.

The shed doesn't look very glamorous, that's for sure. Not much more than a glorified doghouse. I doubt if Architectural Digest will feature it anytime soon.

On the other hand ... it's raining like a bastard outside, but I'm warm and dry. Better yet ... no one is going to rap me awake and tell me to leave. Not in this weather, anyway. I can sleep in peace. Let's hit the sack early tonight.

He undressed, settled into the sleeping bag, and switched off the light.

First night in Casa del Crescendo. Almost like spending the first night with a new girlfriend. Been a long, LONG time since THAT happened.

PART TWO
Cincinnati

IV

The sounds of several different instruments – violins, French horns, oboes, and pianos – filtered into the hallway. It was one of many hallways in Mary Emory Hall, the home of the University of Cincinnati Conservatory of Music. This particular hallway held nothing but practice rooms, each one bleak and featureless, each one occupied by a student musician hard at work. Although the practice rooms came equipped with some measure of soundproofing, the pianist still clearly heard each individual instrument as he walked down the hallway. The sounds annoyed him, as he was trying to find a vacant room, one far away from those occupied, one that would let him practice in relative peace.

Then he heard it. Ravel's "Sonatine," the first movement, coming from one of the rooms. Even with the noise of the other rooms interfering, he stopped in his tracks and listened. He knew the piece, but this performance was unlike anything he'd heard. The notes sounded smoky, and cloudy. Not a single note sounded solid or hard-edged.

That's it! I've always known this is what the piece should sound like! But this is the closest anyone has ever come to that sound!

The first movement ended. He waited a moment, then knocked on the door.

"What?" an annoyed female voice answered.

He opened the door and found a woman with shoulder-length red hair and green eyes. She sat at the keyboard of a Steinway upright.

"I'm … sorry to bother you," he stammered. "But I just wanted to tell you … I've been listening to you play 'Sonatine,' and … my God … you're brilliant."

"Thank you," she replied, with a note of impatience in her voice.

"Well … sorry to bother you," he repeated, then half-bowed as he closed the door.

THAT was stupid! You win the award for the UN-coolest guy on campus.

He retreated to the first open practice room he could find, one that was as far away from the red-haired woman's room as possible. He closed the door and sullenly ran through his warmup routine – scales, and the Hanon. Once finished, he decided to work on Debussy's "Sarabande," the second movement of the "Suite Pour Le Piano."

The Sarabande was one of those pieces that wasn't difficult to play. But it was extremely difficult to play *well*. The slower movement between two up-tempo movements, a change of pace movement, it demanded a great deal of nuance from the pianist. Too many pianists simply played the notes, with feeling whatsoever. Too many others went to the opposite extreme and wound up sounding overwrought and ridiculous.

I'll play the whole piece once, all the way through. Concentrate on the forest, then work on the individual trees.

He finished the piece, paused for a couple of moments, then heard a light knock on the door.

"Come in."

The door opened, and the red-haired woman ducked her head inside.

"Am I interrupting?"

"No," he answered. "Please, come in."

"Thanks. I just wanted to say I'm sorry if I was abrupt with you."

He met her gaze. Her eyes looked like green crystals.

"Quite all right," he answered as smoothly as he could. "I shouldn't have bothered you."

"You didn't. I appreciate what you said. I've been listening to you, too. I love what you did with the Sarabande."

"Thanks," he answered, and was surprised to find his pulse racing. "Are you new here?"

"Yes. First-year grad student. I did my undergrad at John Carroll in Cleveland. How about you?"

"Senior year. You a TA?"

"No. Just a grad student."

"Well … guess we'd better get back to work."

"Guess so."

As she started to back out and close the door, he said, "One thing. When you're done … okay if I walk you home?"

She paused, then said, "I'd like that." He noticed a gap between her two front teeth and found it quite appealing. She wore no makeup, yet her green eyes glowed more intensely with each passing moment.

Her name was Audrey Quigley. She grew up in Orrville, Ohio. Her father worked as a mid-level executive with Smucker's. Her mother, a pianist and organist, gave piano lessons and worked part time at a nearby pipe organ factory. He got that much from her as they navigated the brightly-lit sidewalks that wound through the campus.

"What brings you to Cincy? John Carroll not to your liking?"

"The school was okay," she replied. "Good teachers. But it's a Catholic college, and I could only take so much of the daily Catholicism."

"You Protestant?" he asked.

"No. Atheist."

He laughed and said, "That could be a problem at a Catholic college."

"It certainly was. This is my dorm."

They stopped at a towering, multi-story building with glass doors. He asked, "You live in a dorm?" None of the graduate students he knew lived in a dorm.

"Yes. It's easier for me. I don't want to live off-campus."

"Really? Why's that?" Just about every other student craved the freedom of off-campus living.

"I don't like cities. They make me nervous."

"Oh." He couldn't think of any response to that. He also noticed, for the first time, that she had a bit of a speech impediment. Her Rs sounded vague, almost like Ws. And her Ss came out as SHs.

"Well," she said, "thanks for the walk home."

"My pleasure," he replied. "Thanks for the company."

The next evening, her found her in the hallway of the practice rooms. She wore jeans, a black jacket, and black sneakers. She greeted him with her gap-toothed smile.

"Just the man I was looking for. Do me a favor?"

"Sure."

"Be my guinea-pig audience. Professor Halliday wants me to perform 'Sonatine' before him and two other profs as an exercise. Thing is … I hate performing. Always have. Halliday says I just have to do it more."

He paused, unsure how to respond.

"You hate performing?"

She nodded.

"That's why I'm a composition major. One of the reasons, anyway. Let others have the on-stage agony. All those people *judging* you. And half of them have no idea what music is really about."

"Well, you're right about that. Listen, let's see if the last room at the end is open."

"Why that one?"

"You'll see."

They walked down the hallway until they reached the last room on the right. It was unoccupied.

"The piano in this room is the best," he told her. A black upright Steinway took up most of the tiny room.

"Good to know," she replied.

She removed her black jacket, revealing a loose-fitting light blue blouse.

"Let me warm up a little, okay?"

"Sure."

She sat at the bench. With no other chair in the room, he stood, leaning against the wall. She ran through a couple of the Hanon exercises, then said, "Ready?"

"Ready."

She began the first movement, the *Modere,* with the deceptively simple melody in the right hand, coupled with the sound of a flock of birds rising in the left. A challenge for any pianist, but she again played it with the effortlessness he found so captivating the night before, when the sound of it had stopped him in the hallway.

She finished the first movement, paused, then began the second, the *Menuet.* Like most other minuets, it felt light and breezy – at first. But after about the first ten bars, he began to hear something in her playing, a certain sadness, the disturbing sound of someone hiding a deep unhappiness behind a carefree façade.

The third movement, the *Anime,* disturbed him even more. An energetic, up-tempo piece, with lightning-quick riffs in both the left and right hands, it usually provided pianists with an opportunity to display their bravura virtuosity. But in her hands, the movement sounded jagged, high-strung, and full of what struck him as unfocussed anxiety. The piece ended with an ascending passage that she turned into a soul-baring cry of despair. She held the final chord for several long moments, then dropped her hands into her lap.

He was tempted to leave the room, to distance himself from this troubled woman – until she looked up at him. Her expression seemed soft and vulnerable, hoping for approval, and reflecting none of the harsh darkness he heard in the last movement.

Maybe I'm reading too much into it …

She offered a shy shrug. "Well …?"

He hesitated, then said, "In the hands of a lesser artist, that piece would be merely … *pretty.*"

Her smile grew. He saw traces of an embarrassed blush. The faint red in her cheeks highlighted the green of her eyes.

"Thank you," she said.

"Walk you home again tonight?"

"Sure."

"Feels like it might rain," she said. A humid breeze stirred the tree branches above the sidewalk.

"Yeah, it does."

No sooner had he said it than dark clouds blotted out the quarter-moon.

"Speaking of rain," he said. "Been meaning to tell you something. This may be the most un-artistic analogy possible. But do you remember back in high school, in Driver's Ed, they taught about hydroplaning?"

She shook her head and said, "I didn't take Driver's Ed. I don't drive."

He paused for a moment. *Doesn't drive?*

"Oh," he said. "Well, thing is … if it rains hard enough, a car's tires can lift completely off the road. They just skim along above the water. That's what I thought when I first heard you playing 'Sonatine.'

Sometimes I feel like I'm pushing a truck with four flat tires through the mud. But you sound like you're gliding a foot above the ground, not even touching it."

She turned her face to him, her eyes brightening as if lit by an electric current.

"That's a lovely thing to say. Thanks."

The look in her eyes emboldened him.

"Could I buy you dinner sometime?"

She looked away for a moment, then met his gaze again.

"That's sweet of you to offer. But I don't go to restaurants."

"You don't? Not any?"

"None," she answered. "I'm a vegetarian. I can't stand the sight or smell of meat."

"Oh," he answered. They arrived at the glass front doors of her dorm.

"Well, thanks for seeing me home again," she said. She turned and gave him a hug. It felt, at first, like a polite hug, which was as much as he expected. But then she pulled him close and grasped him tightly. He responded and wound his arms around her. After a moment, she released him, muttered what sounded like an embarrassed "Good night," and half-sprinted to the door.

That's really strange. She hugs you tightly, then runs away. Go figure.

He felt a few raindrops fall and cursed himself for not bringing his umbrella along. But the rain stopped almost as soon as it started.

<hr>

The next day, when he passed her in the hallway, she avoided his eyes.

Well, that's that. She's not the first whacko musician you'll run across. And she won't be the last, either. Flaky musicians are practically the norm around here.

That evening, as he practiced in "the last room on the right," he heard a light knock on the door.

"Come in."

She wore a plain white blouse and jeans. Avoiding his gaze, she said, "Sorry to bother you. Could we talk?"

"Sure."

"I'm sorry I avoided you today."

"That's okay."

"And I'm sorry about last night. I didn't mean to hug you that hard. I guess I just got carried away for a minute."

"Quite all right."

"I just ... don't want you to think I was leading you on, or anything."

"Don't worry about it."

"Thanks." Still not meeting his eyes, she muttered, "You must think I'm a total nut job."

"No, of course not," he lied.

She sighed and said, "Well, I'll let you get back to work."

"No hurry. How did the recital with Halliday go?"

She seemed surprised that he would ask.

"I don't know. Okay, I guess."

He offered a wry smile.

"So, do you like performing now?"

She laughed and shook her head.

"No!"

"Didn't think so."

She stayed silent for a moment, then half-whispered, "Walk me home again tonight?"

"Sure."

***

After walking her home, he returned to his off-campus apartment, poured himself a glass of Cabernet Sauvignon, flopped onto his couch, and brooded.

This is not a good idea. I've made it through three years of the conservatory without getting into a relationship. It's been tough at times, but that's the life of a music student. It's like a monastic existence, giving up almost all of your life in the service of music.

That life would be a lot tougher if you tried to balance a full academic workload, hours of practice every day, and a relationship. Add to it the fact that she's obviously got some problems. And you may have only seen her smaller problems.

And yet ... there is something undeniably intriguing about her. She's not beautiful. Her nose is too big and wide, and her chin was a bit too prominent. But those eyes. A brilliant pianist, she is terrified of performing, yet brings the heart of a poet to her playing. She mixes moments of soaring, stunning beauty with jagged passages that seem to reveal a deeply troubled soul. She lives a musical hermit's life, never venturing beyond the campus, spending all of her time either at the conservatory or in her dorm room.

Maybe she has the right idea, after all. That's the way a music student should live. The single-minded devotion of a monk. Or a nun. Odd, how she hated the Catholic life at John Carroll, yet seems perfectly suited for the spartan life of a Jesuit.

He stood, walked over to his record cabinet, and removed an LP, "French Keyboard Masterpieces," by Ivan Moravec. He fired up his turntable and amplifier, plugged in his headphones, and dropped the stylus onto the first track of Side A. Ravel's "Sonatine."

His piano teacher introduced him to the piece when he was in high school. At the teacher's suggestion, his mother bought him the Moravec LP a short time later. Since then, he'd heard several pianists perform "Sonatine," but Moravec's version remained his favorite. Until now.

He sat and listened to the piece all the way through, sipping his Cabernet. When the piece ended, he replaced the LP in the sleeve, shut down the stereo … and thought of something. He crossed over to his phone stand and opened the Cincinnati Yellow Pages.

The next evening, he found her in their favored practice room.

"Hey, there," she greeted him. "Want to be a guinea pig-audience again?"

"Sure. What's the occasion this time?"

"I just finished a new piece. Not sure yet what it is. I call it 'Something or Other in C-Minor.'"

"Love to hear it."

She sat at the Steinway and began playing. Like her version of "Sonatine," the piece had no square edges. It was all smoky chords and enigmatic melody lines. The two sometimes blurred, with the chord progressions an integral part of the melody.

He found one segment absolutely captivating. She played what sounded like a fourth, lowered it to the major third, repeated the fourth, then lowered it to a *minor* third. That chord progression gave him goosebumps. He almost levitated.

She finished, dropped her hands in her lap, then gazed at him with a bright glow in her eyes.

"What do you think?"

"It's … great. It doesn't seem to have any … solidity. Just smoke and clouds."

She looked down for a moment, then briefly met his gaze.

"Thanks."

"That one progression – the fourth, lowered to a major third, then the minor. Could you play that again?"

"Sure."

She played the four-bar segment again. He followed her hands, and saw it was an F-Minor 7 to E-Flat Major, followed by an F-Seventh to E-Flat *Minor,* with the F moving to G-Flat in the bass line. Then she repeated the F-Minor 7 to E-Flat Major, and finished with a B-Flat Major to A-Flat Major.

"Wow," he said. "That is … just … how on earth did you come up with that?"

She grinned and said, "Accidentally. I meant to just repeat the first two chords."

"It's … I've never heard anything like it. So … you don't know what the piece is?"

"Not yet."

"Just my two cents. I think it would make a good second movement of a piano sonata."

"Really?"

"Really. Have you written any other pieces that might make good first or third movements?"

She averted her eyes again, stared at the piano keys, and mumbled, "I don't know. Maybe."

"Good. Meanwhile, I want to ask you something. Ever hear of Mischa Dichter?"

"No."

"Pianist. Really great. He's performing Rachmaninoff's Second this Saturday with the Cincinnati Symphony. Wanna go?"

She continued to gaze at the piano keys.

"Are you … asking me out on a date?"

"Well … I'm going anyway, and I just thought … yeah, I guess so. One other thing. The concert is at two. Afterwards, we could head over to a vegetarian restaurant I found."

She looked up, her eyes widening.

"A *vegetarian* restaurant? You sure?"

"I'm sure. Cincy's a restaurant town. You can find at least one of everything."

"Where?"

"A few blocks away from the Music Hall."

"You're sure they're totally vegetarian?"

"Yeah. I called and asked. No meat anywhere in sight."

"I don't know … I told you I don't do well in cities."

"I'll be with you the whole time."

"How will we get there?"

"We can take a cab."

"No. I can't handle cabs."

"How about if I rent a car? That work?"

"Well … I guess."

"Great. Pick you up at one o'clock?"

"Okay."

He had trouble sleeping that night. Shortly after midnight, he got up and went to his piano. He played the four-bar phrase several times, and thought it was unlike anything he'd ever heard. And that made a type of sense, because Audrey was unlike anyone he'd ever met.

She stayed silent during the ride to the Music Hall. Not just silent, but hunched and tense, as if she were trying, with all her might, to control her anxiety. When they walked to and from the parking garage near the Music Hall, she gripped his arm tightly, and not, he knew, out of affection.

She still squeezed his arm as he led her to the vegetarian restaurant. Once inside, she relaxed slightly.

"This place is amazing," she said as they settled into a walnut booth. "How did you find it?"

"The Yellow Pages."

"Really? They actually advertise vegetarian restaurants?"

"They actually do. You're not the only vegetarian in town."

"Feels like it, sometimes," she said.

He almost replied *You ought to get out more,* but decided *that's too harsh. Easy does it, now. Still trying to figure her out.*

"I love the décor," she said.

"Yeah." It was what he expected from an oh-so-hip vegetarian joint — bare brick walls, exposed ceiling beams and ducting, hardwood floors, potted plants, and a slate chalkboard listing the daily specials.

He thought Audrey looked better than ever. She wore a canary-yellow blouse that set off her red hair and green eyes, along with a black skirt, black flats, and no stockings. For some reason, he found her unstockinged legs quite provocative.

Girl's legs aren't bad, not one damn bit!

The waitress, a pale-skinned young woman with blue hair, brought their menus. Audrey opened hers and began reading in wide-eyed wonder. He said nothing, letting her absorb her first experience at a vegetarian restaurant.

"The menu's impressive," she said.

"Sure is,' he replied. "I was expecting cardboard and bird seed."

She laughed, the first real laugh he'd heard from her, a graceless, honking guffaw that he found as appealing as her gap-toothed smile. She seemed to fully relax for the first time.

Scanning his menu, he found something intriguing – a sandwich called a "PLT." Just like a BLT, but with smoked, deep-fried potato skins in lieu of bacon.

The blue-haired waitress reappeared. Audrey ordered an eggplant-and-tofu chow mein. He ordered the PLT and a cup of tomato-basil soup. As the waitress departed, he told Audrey, "I think my father might actually approve of this place."

"How so?"

"Typical engineer. He gets completely worked up over the smallest things. One of them was potato skins. He told us – over and OVER – how stupid it is to throw away the skins. They're the most nutritious part of the potato."

"Well, I suppose he's right about that."

"I know. That's what was so annoying."

She laughed again and asked, "Do you and your father get along?"

He gave a slight grimace.

"Not always."

"He against you being a pianist?"

"No. He was okay with it once he admitted I wasn't cut out to be an engineer. That was the problem. Still is."

"I'm sorry."

"How about you?"

"My folks are okay," she said with a slight roll of her eyes. "They just think I'm weird. And they're right. I am."

"What'd they expect? You're a musician. We're all whackos. That's a given."

She giggled and said, "Thanks for saying that. Makes me feel a little better."

He saw a new look in her eyes. The usual electric-green intensity gave way to a softer, warmer look he found enchanting.

The waitress brought their orders. Audrey took one bit of her chow mein and nearly shouted, "Mmmm! *Mmmm!* Oh, this is *great!*"

"How long have you been a vegetarian?" he asked.

"Four years. Oh, GOD this is good!" Her loud voice caused some of the other diners to turn their heads and stare at her.

"Four years, and you've never been to a restaurant? Just preparing your own food?"

"Yeah, pretty much. OH, this is great!"

It's almost as if she's discovering food for the first time. Hard to believe she never knew that vegetarian restaurants actually existed. Hell, I'm not veg, but even I knew they were out there.

He took a bite out of his sandwich and tasted a pleasant surprise. The smoked potato skins came seasoned with garlic, onion salt, paprika, and a few other herbs he didn't immediately recognize. The dark brown bread was heavier and coarser than he preferred, but had a rich, grainy flavor. The tomato-basil soup was perfect in its simplicity.

They spoke little while they ate. She obviously savored every bite, and he wanted to let her enjoy the experience.

She finished her chow mein, leaned back in her chair and sighed, "That was just the *best!* Thanks so much for finding this! Now I want to try every other item on the menu."

"Glad you liked it," he answered. Now that she seemed more relaxed, he asked her, "What did you think of Mischa?"

"Wow," she exhaled. "He was great! Best thing about him ... he made the third movement sound really powerful, but without being melodramatic, like everyone else does."

"I agree. Everyone else plays the third movement like it's the pop song version." He sang, "Full Moooon .... And Emmmmpty Arrrmmmssss ..."

She responded with a blank look.

"There's a pop song version of it?"

"Yeah," he replied. "Sinatra sang it, and several others."

"Never heard it."

"Several classical pieces were turned into pop songs," he told her. "Borodin's 'Polovtzian Dances' became 'Stranger in Paradise.' Debussy's 'Reverie' was turned into 'My Reverie.' Some others."

She glowered and said, "Awful. Turning great music into pop garbage."

They ordered dessert, which consisted of two graham crackers with a peanut butter filling, covered with a dark chocolate coating. Between bites, they talked music. Her knowledge of classical music was almost encyclopedic. On the other hand, she knew very little about jazz, and damn near nothing about popular music.

The waitress brought the check. He told Audrey, "Well, guess we ought to be getting home."

"Do you really think classical and popular music can mix?" she asked, as streetlights passed in waves over the car.

"Don't see why not," he answered. "The Broadway composers – Gershwin, Rogers, Kern – were all classically trained. Even the old Brill Building song pluggers."

"What about rock musicians?"

"Some of them are. The good ones, anyway."

"Mmmh," she grunted.

"The problem isn't the musicians. It's the record companies. Sometimes they need a good song in a hurry, and decide it's just easier and quicker to rip off a classical piece and stick some cheesy lyrics onto it. They figure most people are too musically illiterate to know the difference. And most of the time, they're right."

"Mmmh," she grunted again.

"Listen, you don't have to do this if you don't want to, but – if you'd like – want to come over to my place? For just a bit? I have some examples of rock musicians who are fairly well-schooled."

She remained silent for several long moments, then said, "Okay."

He sat in his easy chair. She sat on his couch, in his living room, one of two rooms and a kitchen that made up his second-floor apartment. Between them, his walnut coffee table held several CD cases and LP album covers. On his turntable, the last few measures of "Dust in the Wind" by Kansas faded away.

He stole a glance at her stocking-less legs, then stood. He moved the stylus back to the mount and shut the turntable off.

"What do you think?" he asked.

"You're right, the violin-viola duet is good," she said. "Depressing lyrics, though."

"Maybe," he replied, stealing another glance. "Maybe they're just telling people to not be overly impressed with themselves. We both know plenty of people in this school who could use that advice."

She grinned and said, "That's true. Listen, I really should be going."

"Sure. Thanks for everything."

"Thank you. I had a great time."

Her grin vanished. She said, "I have to tell you something. Please don't be mad at me."

"Go ahead."

She gazed at the coffee table.

"You're really nice. But I … don't think we should do this again. I'm putting everything I have into music and can't allow myself any luxuries. Even something as harmless as a dinner date."

"I understand," he said. "I guess I feel the same way. If you want to succeed, music has to be your whole life. Nothing else can interfere."

"Thanks. Sure you're not mad at me?"

"I'm sure."

"Good," she sighed. "Glad we got that out of the way."

"Me, too."

They stood. Her gaze met his. He moved one step closer to her. She moved a step closer to him. He felt pulled toward her, unable to resist, and knew for certain she felt the same pull. They opened their arms to each other, embraced, and kissed. Her mouth felt wonderfully soft and sweet.

After several long moments, they drew apart. She reached behind her waist for his hands. He felt crestfallen – she was backing away. But then she grasped his hands and brought them up to the top button of her yellow blouse.

"All of them," she whispered, her lower lip quivering.

⸻

She snuggled next to him and pulled the white sheet up to their shoulders. Her head rested on his left shoulder. A steady rain pattered against his bedroom window.

"How did that happen?" she asked.

"I don't know. You having second thoughts?"

"No. But I don't do one-night stands."

"Neither do I."

"I like you a lot," she said. "But what I said is still true. The time we spend with each other is time away from what we should be doing."

"I know. We understand each other. Maybe too well. We both know how lonely a musician's life can be. Especially the student years. Just when you most need someone to care about you is the time … when you can't allow yourself that luxury."

"So … what are we going to do?"

He thought for a few moments.

"How about this? We make absolutely no demands on each other's time. We both know music has to come first."

"Okay. What else?"

"Remember when you said you wanted to sample every dish on the menu?"

"Yeah."

"Once a week, max, we have dinner together, either at today's restaurant or one of the other vegetarian joints. Afterwards, we spend a few hours with each other. We won't cut into our practicing or studying time. But we provide each other with the physical affection we both need. Maybe take the sting out of the loneliness."

She propped herself up on her right elbow.

"Do you really think it can work that way?"

He nodded. "Yeah, I think so. Here's why. I know damn well that if I told someone, 'Audrey and I are in bed together because we have so much respect for each other as musicians,' they'd laugh. But it's the truth. One of the reasons, anyway. We both know what a long haul we're facing. We think highly of each other. We care about each other. And we can help each other."

"So … how long do you think this will last?"

He grinned and said, "Until you get tired of me and give me the boot."

She offered a sad smile and said, "That won't happen."

"Don't be so sure. You've yet to learn how much of a pain in the ass I can be. But anyway … you can back out anytime you want."

"Okay. Anything else?"

"Yeah. Have you ever heard of W.H. Auden and Christopher Isherwood?"

"No."

"Couple of British writers. Both gay. I once read an article that described them as sometime lovers and lifelong friends. We can be a straight version of them. How long will we last? I hope all our lives. Whether we do *this* or not, we'll always care about each other."

"Sometime lovers and lifelong friends," she repeated. Then she grinned and said, "So, other than respecting me so damn much, are there any other reasons why you want to be in bed with me?"

"Sure," he answered. "You're beautiful."

"Come on," she growled, her grin disappearing. "I know I'm not."

"Yes, you are. You have the most beautiful eyes I've ever seen."

She lowered her head until her nose and forehead touched his. She whispered, "So do you."

V

The following Monday, they encountered each other in the hallway. He fought the urge to publicly embrace and kiss her, and guessed she fought the same urges.

"I took your advice," she said.

"How so?"

"I have a couple of other pieces I've been kicking around. Didn't really know what to do with them. But when you said my C-Minor piece would make a good second movement, I went back and dug the other two out of my filing cabinet. I spent all day Sunday working on them. I think I may have a piano sonata in the works."

"Great!" he told her. "Can't wait to hear it."

"You'll be the first," she told him.

"Mmmm," she purred.

"I get the feeling you're starting to like this," he teased.

She giggled and said, "What makes you say that?"

"Oh, I'm psychic," he said. "I can read your mind."

She nestled the top of her head into his neck. He couldn't see her face, but could tell she was smiling.

"One of your many talents," she said.

They'd spent the day per their agreement. Both practiced piano in the afternoon for about four hours. Then they drove over to the same vegetarian restaurant. She tried out a slightly different dish – tofu and eggplant with brown rice, which she also loved. He stayed with his PLT sandwich. When they returned to his apartment they moved immediately into the bedroom.

The two of them snuggled silently for a few more moments. Then she said, "Ask you something?"

"Sure."

"When you were in school … were you popular?"

"I had my circle of friends. Musicians, and the other arty kids. The rest
– the jocks, the cheerleaders, the 'In-Crowd' … I didn't care about."

"You really didn't care?"

"No."

"Why not?"

He grinned.

"Just a guess, but I think it's because of my colossal, monstrous ego."

She burst out laughing.

"You're so funny."

"I'm totally serious."

She laughed harder.

He pulled her close with both arms, hugged her, kissed the top of her
head, and asked, "How about you?"

He felt her tense up.

"No."

"Any idea why?"

"Yeah," she answered. "You probably noticed I have a speech
impediment?"

"It's not bad," he told her.

"It was. When I was younger. Really bad. Plus, I had a stutter. The
other kids in first grade noticed it right away. I was shy to begin with, and
then they started in on me, making fun of the way I spoke. It just got
worse after that. They made fun of everything about me. How I spoke,
how I dressed. How fat I was. Called me names like Oddball Audrey. By
the time I got to high school, I didn't even try to make friends. Didn't
know how, didn't know what they wanted. I just kept to myself and my
piano."

"Kids are supposed to be so innocent," he said. "They're not."

"Never understood why they hated me so much," she said. "What did
I ever do to them?"

"Nothing," he said. "It's not you. It's them. They were mean to you
because they were mean. They were the ones with the problem. Not you."

She said nothing. But after a few moments, he felt her sweet body start
to shake in his embrace. Warm, wet tears flowed onto his left shoulder.

"I just wish I knew what was wrong with me," she sobbed.

He stroked her arm and said, "I can think of a million things that are *right* about you."

Her body shook harder. More tears poured onto his shoulder. He held her and rocked her, back and forth, back and forth …

When he awoke the next morning, the pale blue predawn light spilled through his bedroom window. The sight of her lying next to him gave him a brief shock. This was only their second night together, and he was still not used to waking up to a companion.

She lay asleep on her side, facing him. He took a few moments to gaze at her.

Her breasts were fairly small. Yet he still found them appealing. Small or not, they appeared to him as perfectly shaped pearls. Her hips, on the other hand, were a bit on the wide side, but also not unattractive.

Small of bust, wide of hip. The exact opposite of what we're supposed to want. Her body is like the rest of her, somehow beautiful in its own undefinable way.

She yawned, sighed, opened her eyes … and sat bolt upright. Her head snapped back and forth. He took her hand.

"It's okay," he told her. "You're with me."

She relaxed and collapsed back onto the mattress.

"Whew! Sorry, didn't know where I was for a minute."

"Takes a little getting used to."

"Thanks. How long have you been awake?"

"Couple of minutes." He stroked her forearm and teased, "I've just been enjoying the view."

She giggled and covered her eyes with her hands.

"Hope you weren't disappointed."

"Just the opposite," he said. "I could enjoy this view all day."

She buried her face into the pillow and said, "Oh, stop."

He put his face next to hers and said, "Come out, come out, wherever you are …"

She removed her face from the pillow and turned her green eyes to him.

"Why are you so good to me?" she whispered.

"Why not? You're awfully good to me."

They kissed for a few moments. Then she said, "Hate to break the mood, but I need to use your bathroom."

"Of course," he said. "One of the privileges of being my honored guest."

She giggled and hopped out of the bed. His eyes followed her as she crossed the room and opened the bathroom door. A few moments later, she reappeared and flopped back into bed next to him, burying her forehead in the left side of his neck.

"Not yet six AM," she said, her left hand resting on his chest. "You need to be anywhere soon?"

"No. Matter of fact, I was thinking … this is one of the advantages to spending Saturday night with an atheist. They don't have to rush off on Sunday morning."

She laughed. "Got that right." She removed her forehead from his neck, rolled onto her back, smiled at him, and said, "Let's …"

They kept their routine of walking together every night from Mary Emory Hall to her dorm room. Their walk came only after their practicing was done.

On the next Wednesday night, as they approached her dorm, she told him, "I almost forgot. I can't make dinner this Saturday. My parents are coming down Friday to visit."

"Rats," he replied. He almost asked her if she wanted to move their dinner date up to Thursday. But then he remembered what he told her. *Once a week, max. Music comes first.*

"You tell your parents about me?" he asked.

"Not yet. I think I will. Not all of it, though," she said through a nervous giggle.

"Probably best not to tell all."

They walked together in silence for several moments. Then he said, "Ask you something?"

"Sure."

"How come you never wear any makeup?"

She scowled and said, "I never saw the point to it. We're supposed to spend all this time and money on stuff that just makes us look painted up and freakish. Not real at all. Why bother?"

"Well … done right, it can make a beautiful woman look even more beautiful."

"Psshhh. If it's so great, why don't men use it?"

"Wouldn't help. We'd still be ugly."

She stayed silent for a moment, then laughed her awkward, honking laugh.

"Men aren't ugly!"

"Sure we are. Come on. Women are works of art. Men are like tow trucks. We serve our purpose, but we ain't much to look at."

She laughed again, then said, "My mom used to get on my case all the time for not wearing makeup. Said it make me look like a lesbian."

He grinned at her.

"If she only knew."

She gave another high-strung giggle as they arrived at her dorm's large glass front door.

"Well, if you really don't like wearing it, then don't," he told her. "You're beautiful enough without it."

She gazed at him. The streetlights seemed to make her eyes glow more brightly.

"Know something?" she asked.

"What?"

"You're almost making me believe it."

He smiled at her and said, "Progress marches on."

They embraced and kissed. It occurred to him this was the first time they'd ever kissed outdoors, in the presence of others. A few people passed by but took little notice of the two of them. He realized, with a sense of wry disappointment, that they were not that special. Kissing couples were a common sight on the campus.

He spent that Saturday practicing morosely in their favorite room. He tried to concentrate on Debussy's "Sarabande" and "Passepied," but found himself bitterly resenting her parents. *Why did they have to come and visit this weekend? The holidays are coming up, why couldn't they wait until then?*

The next weekend also proved to be a disappointment. She called him that morning and apologized, saying she had a terrible cramps that were lasting longer than normal.

"I'm sorry," he said. "Can I bring you anything?"

"No, but thank you for offering," she said.

"A friend once mentioned that red wine can help."

"Thanks. But I don't drink any alcohol."

"Oh," he replied, and thought *I should have known.*

The next weekend was Thanksgiving, and both were home visiting their families.

She phoned the following weekend, saying she had come down with the flu. He was beginning to fear she was looking for excuses not to see him. But then he, too, came down with the flu, and learned several other students and faculty members were also afflicted. Even though the fever and chills were awful, he actually felt better for it, knowing that she was not avoiding him.

The next weekend, both were well enough to keep their date. He had a surprise in store for her. Over Thanksgiving, his Uncle Max helped him to buy a car, a used Toyota Corolla in good condition. From now on, he would be able to take her to dinner in his own car, not a rental.

The Saturday was sunny and bitterly cold, about ten degrees above zero. He pulled into the parking lot next to her dorm and was surprised to find her waiting for him. He almost didn't recognize her. Along with a heavy overcoat, she wore a knit cap, large sunglasses, and a scarf wound around her neck and mouth.

He opened the door for her and started to hug her. She held up her hand and said, "Wait. I have a surprise for you. Close your eyes."

He closed his eyes and turned his head to the left for good measure. After several moments, she said, "Okay. You can look now."

He opened his eyes, turned his head back to her … and gasped.

She wore … makeup. Not too much, but just enough. Light blush on her cheeks and bright red lipstick. Black eye liner and medium eye shadow, both of which made her green eyes seem even larger and more enchanting.

"WOW! Where …?"

"I asked the woman who does my hair. She did it all. I told her you always say such nice things about my eyes. She said to tell you … 'Got that damn right!'"

"Wow," he repeated. "She did a great job. You look fantastic!"

She laughed, another graceless but warm laugh, and said, "You idiot."

"You look great. Just great."

She looked away for a moment, then met his gaze, her eyes glowing.

"Listen, before we go to dinner … could we go to your place first?"

"Mmmm," she purred, nestling in next to him. "Twice in one day."

They were back in his bed after a later-than-usual dinner.

"Mmmm," he agreed.

"Still can't believe I did that," she said.

"Did what?"

"Wore that makeup out in public. Couple of times, I almost went to the ladies' room to wipe it all off. Felt ridiculous, like I was trying to be a fashion model or something. I was sure everyone in the restaurant was laughing at me."

"They weren't laughing," he said.

"Sure?"

"Sure. You were the hottest babe in the joint. Every other woman wanted to look like you. They wanted to BE you."

She buried her face in his chest and giggled, "I don't think so."

"I KNOW so. Something else. Every man in the restaurant took one look at you … and wanted to be ME!"

She giggled harder and said, "Oh stop it, will you?"

He grinned and said, "No."

VI

The following Thursday, just after noon, she caught up with him in the hallway and said, "Be my guinea-pig audience again tonight?"

"Sure. What's the occasion?"

"You'll see."

That night, after he finished dinner, he found her in their practice room.

"Guinea Pig reporting as ordered, sir," he teased.

"Thanks," she said with a smile. She was back to her no-makeup mode. He was disappointed at first, but then decided he liked her no-makeup mode just fine.

"What do you have?" he asked.

"Remember 'Something or Other in C-Minor?'"

"You bet."

She sighed a nervous sigh.

"Okay. I finished the whole sonata. Want to hear it?"

"Love to."

"Thanks. Three movements – *Allegro, Andante,* and *Vivace.*"

She began playing the first movement, a swift, up-tempo piece. He again thought she sounded like a hydroplaning car – gliding effortlessly, not touching the ground. Gradually, she gained intensity, until she sounded as if she were desperately trying to attain something elusive.

The second movement, the *Andante,* a slower piece, sounded very much in the mode of Ravel or Debussy – all smoke and clouds, no sharp edges, with the wonderful F7 to E-Flat progression he'd heard before.

The *Vivace* shocked him. A fast, furious piece, she played it with a sense of confidence and verve he'd never heard from her. In contrast to the jagged, unfocussed anger he heard from her in "Sonatine," she now seemed to roar pride and defiance at the world. He thought it was a lovely sound.

She finished, held the last chord until it died, then dropped her hands into her lap. Gazing at the keyboard, she whispered, "Well …?"

He took a few moments before replying.

"I don't use the word 'genius' carelessly," he told her. "You're a genius."

Her hands shot up, covering her eyes.

"You ..." she said, then halted.

"Listen, I know you hate performing. But have you ever done any recording? We really need to have some sort of record of what you can do."

She lowered her hands, reached into her purse, and pulled out a tissue. Wiping her eyes, she said, "Not really. Maybe it might not be a bad idea."

"Let's work on it."

She finished wiping her eyes and said, "Okay. Now, something I keep forgetting to ask. Do you have any plans after graduation?"

He nodded. "Yeah. Ever hear of Berklee College of Music?

"No."

"There's a saying about conservatories. 'They teach you everything about music except how to make a living at it.' Berklee teaches you how to make a living at it, how to be a working musician."

"Such as?"

"Writing pop songs. Recording them. Producing records. Composing and recording film scores and music for TV commercials. Things like that."

"You'd really want to do those things?"

"That's how you subsidize the music you want to do. The alternative is selling insurance."

"Are you sure you don't want to be a concert pianist?"

"Tough racket," he told her. "Talent is just half of what you need. Lot of politics with symphonies."

"Where is Berklee?"

"Boston."

"Boston," she repeated. "And after that?"

"New York or LA. Probably LA. How about you?"

She stared at the keyboard and said, "I don't know. Maybe teaching at a small college somewhere."

The two of them said nothing for several moments. Then she murmured, "Guess we should get back to work. Thanks for listening."

"Thanks for asking."

The next day, a Friday, she was nowhere in sight. He hoped she wasn't getting sick again. On Saturday morning, she called him at his apartment.

"I'm sorry," she said, her voice sounding dry and rough. "I can't be with you today."

"Are you okay?" he asked, alarmed by the sound of her voice.

"I'm having a bad day. I just … can't face anything."

"Is there anything I can do?"

"No. I don't even know what the problem is. I just … get like this sometimes."

"Let me know if I can help."

"I will. Thanks."

She hung up. He replaced the receiver in its cradle and poured himself a glass of milk.

Hope she's okay. Wish I knew what the problem is.

On Monday night, he found her in their practice room at the end of the hallway. He waited until she took a break, then knocked on the door.

"Hi," he said.

"Hi."

"How are you?"

"Okay, I guess. I'm really sorry."

"No need to apologize," he said.

"I warned you I was weird."

"No, you're not."

"I wouldn't blame you if you dumped me."

"I'm not going to."

"Thing is … I really wanted to see you. But I was a basket case, and didn't want to inflict all that on you."

"It's okay."

She sighed and said, "I just wish I knew what was wrong with me."

He paused. "I'm no shrink. You don't have to pay any attention to anything I say. But I've heard of other people who have the same thing happen to them. They get so they can't leave their rooms. Seems like it happens most often to really brilliant, creative people. What happened on Saturday might just be something that goes with the territory."

She offered a sad smile.

"Does that ever happen to you?"

"No," he said. "But I'm not brilliant."

She gave a small laugh and said, "Oh, yes you are."

"Uh-uh. Not like you. Not even close."

Gazing at the keyboard, she said, "Okay if I ask a favor?"

"Sure."

She brought her eyes up and met his gaze.

"I know it's not Saturday. But could we break the rules and spend tonight together?"

"Absolutely."

"Thing is … I don't know if I'm up for sex. Could I just … be with you?"

"Sure."

The holidays flew by in a flash. When they ended, he and Audrey quickly returned to their regular routines. Both carried a full academic load, and both were committed to hours of grinding daily practice. They permitted themselves their two ongoing indulgences. Every night, when they finished practicing, he drove her back through the bitter cold to her dorm room. On Saturdays, they practiced for several hours in the morning and afternoon, then made time for each other in the evening.

But he soon coaxed her into leaving the campus early on Saturday mornings and venturing out into the city with him. During the first week of January, he took her to the Cincinnati Art Museum to see an exhibit of early French Impressionist paintings. To his delight, she immediately grasped the similarities between Impressionist painting and Impressionist music. In the weeks that followed, they took in performances of the ballet, opera, and symphony. One week he even managed to talk her into attending a jazz concert. Gradually, baby-step by baby-step, she seemed to feel more relaxed in the city.

In the evenings, they dined at one of the vegetarian restaurants, then returned to his second-story apartment, where they listened to music, occasionally watched a movie, and made sweet, soaring love.

They snuggled together on his couch, listening to his LP of Ralph Sutton playing Bix Beiderbecke's piano pieces. He'd told her about Bix. How, along with Louis Armstrong, Bix was one of the great jazz cornetists of the twenties. How Bix also played piano and wanted to compose classical pieces. How he completed four works for piano before he drank himself to death at age 28.

"So sad," she said. "Any idea why he drank so much?"

"Hard to say. Bix was really strange. Absent-minded, irresponsible. Friends say he seemed to exist in his own world and had no end of trouble with the real world."

She shook her head.

"Another weird musician."

He knew what she meant and told her, "At least you're smart enough to stay away from alcohol."

"Thanks. But you were right. This helps."

"How so?

"I'm working harder than ever and getting more done. All because I have ... this ... to look forward to. Being with you isn't getting in the way of music. It's making it easier."

"Good."

"I didn't even realize how lonely I was."

"Me, neither."

"It hurt. Physically hurt."

"Yeah."

The last notes of Bix's "Flashes" faded away. He stood, placed the LP back in its sleeve, and shut the stereo off. He returned to the couch and they resumed their snuggling. Her head rested on his shoulder.

"I almost forgot," she said. "I need to ask another favor."

"Shoot."

"The Composition majors have their recitals coming up. Any chance you could play my C-Minor Sonata?"

He paused and said, "Not sure I could do it justice."

"Sure you could."

"Sounds a whole lot better when you play it."

She shook her head.

"You know I can't do that."

"Maybe you can."

"I hate performing."

"You did great playing it for me."

"That's different."

"Think of them as a guinea pig audience. Only instead of one, you have a whole recital hall's worth."

She laughed softly and said, "Lotta pigs."

"You know, every time I listen to you play, I think what a shame it is that so many people never get the chance to hear you."

She hugged him tightly and murmured, "Well … maybe …"

The next Monday, he spoke with his friend Lou, who ran the recording studio, and booked two hours for Audrey.

In addition to Sonata in C-Minor, she decided to record three preludes that she had "knocked out," along with "Sonatine" and Satie's "Gnossienes." She recorded all of them on the first take except her Sonata. She fussed and fretted her way through four takes before she was satisfied.

That night, as he drove her home, she told him, "Okay. I think I'll go ahead and perform on Composer's Night."

"Great."

They drove in silence along the cold, snowy road for a few moments. Then he asked, "What will you wear?"

She snorted and said, "Oh, hell, I don't know. Who cares?"

"Makes a difference," he said.

"How? Will it make me play better?"

"Maybe," he said. "Lots of things can have subconscious effects. What you're wearing, who's in the audience, where you're playing. Besides, is there a law that says you can't look good and sound good at the same time?"

"Stupid," she muttered.

"Tell you what," he said, "Okay if I pick something out for you?"

She rolled her eyes and muttered, "I don't know. I guess."

Just after lunch the next day, he called his sister. After the requisite chat about their parents, he told her, "Need to ask a favor."

"Shoot."

"A friend has a recital coming up. She needs an evening gown. Stereotypical female pianist. Totally brilliant. Zero fashion sense."

"What's her body type?"

"Slim build. About five-four, five-five or so."

"She busty?"

"Not really."

"Hair and eye color?"

"Coppery red hair. Shade of a brand-new penny. Green eyes."

His sister thought for a moment.

"Go with celadon. It'll set off her hair. Look for a criss-cross top."

"Any chance you could go with us?"

"Sorry, no, I have a conference this weekend. Take her over to Drake's. It's on Bridal Way in Downtown."

"Will do. Thanks."

He dragged her over to Drake's on a Saturday afternoon. A gray-haired, middle-aged saleswoman greeted them and said to Audrey, "What may I help you with?"

He answered, "We'd like to see a celadon evening gown with a criss-cross top."

The saleswoman looked a big confused, and more than a little disapproving, over the fact that he had answered rather than Audrey. But she helped them locate a floor-length celadon gown with a criss-cross top and a knee-high slit on the left side. Audrey disappeared into the fitting room for a few moments.

When she reappeared, he gasped. So did the saleswoman.

"You look great!" he said. "Take a look in the mirror!"

Audrey did so and muttered, "I guess it'll do. No frills or other dopey fru-fru."

The saleswoman told Audrey, "We'll need to make some alterations. Can you pick up the gown next week?"

Audrey nodded and said, "Yeah."

On the drive back home, he said, "One other thing. When you pick up the gown next week, you'll want to take it over to the woman who does your hair and makeup. That way, she'll be able to match the makeup to the gown."

"Okay," she grumped.

The two of them rode in silence for several minutes. Then Audrey said, "I still don't know why I need to do any of this."

"Well … you don't *need* to," he answered. "But outfits like this are part of the whole picture. Some performances are formal affairs, and you have to dress for the occasion."

"These gowns are pretty damn uncomfortable," she said. "We'd play a lot better wearing normal clothes. Besides, do men have to get all fancied up like this?"

"Well, we have to wear tuxedoes. Believe me, those penguin outfits can be pretty damn uncomfortable, too."

She stayed silent for a few moments, then broke out into her honking laugh.

"Penguin outfits! I never heard that!"

He said, "All things considered, I think you'll look better in the gown than in a penguin outfit."

"Maybe. But not by much."

He paused, then gently asked, "You really don't know how beautiful you are, do you?"

Her smile vanished. She shook her head and said, "I've never felt like it. No one ever told me. They all just made fun of me for being fat and weird."

"You're definitely not fat anymore. When did that change?"

"When I went vegetarian. I didn't just give up meat. I gave up all junk food. That got rid of the pounds."

"Smart move."

"Thanks."

He reached over, took her hand, and told her, "But you can take it from me — you are beautiful. After all, I'm a card-carrying heterosexual male. We're experts on that subject."

She laughed and squeezed his hand. A few moments later, she started sobbing, softly.

The two of them stood in the backstage waiting room. All the other composers had gone before her.

"You look great," he told her. He meant it. As he suggested, she took the gown to her hair stylist. Once again, her stylist did her makeup for her and did a masterful job — just enough, but not too much. Foundation, eye liner, a touch of blush, and medium eye shadow. The makeup perfectly complimented the colors of her gown, hair, and eyes.

"You need to tell your stylist — she outdid herself. You are HER senior recital!"

She gave a high-strung giggle and said, "I'll tell her."

He wasn't the only one who liked the way she looked. The other three composers on the program — one man and two women — all offered gushing compliments. The women trilled, "I've never SEEN you look so beautiful!" The man, a pudgy, balding guy named Ward, gracelessly blurted, "Holy SHIT! Audrey! I didn't know it was you!"

She stood, too nervous to sit, her shoulders and neck hunched forward. He thought she looked like Davey Concepcion at shortstop, crouching and waiting for a wicked grounder. She drummed her fingers on a wooden desk. He guessed she was playing one of the Hanon exercises, but without a keyboard.

"I just hope I don't trip over this damn thing and fall on my face."

"I'll pick you up if you do."

"Psshh."

They heard the faint sound of applause coming from the auditorium. Ward had finished.

"Your turn," he said with an encouraging smile. He took her hand and led her out to the wings.

"Okay, remember … back straight, shoulders squared. Give them a Miss America smile and bow."

She gave a brittle nod.

"The non-verbal message you're sending is …'I'm way hotter than any a you bitches.'"

She giggled and kissed his cheek.

"Thanks," she whispered. With great effort, she arched her back, squared her shoulders, and walked onto the stage. He heard a collective gasp from the audience.

Good! The gown and the makeup have done their jobs!

The audience broke into applause. Her back was turned to him, so he couldn't tell if she remembered to smile. But he watched as she bowed and took her place on the Steinway grand's piano bench.

She began the first movement, the Allegro. He winced. She was obviously very nervous, and sounded heavy-handed and laborious as she squeezed out the notes. He heard none of the effortless hydroplaning he'd found so exhilarating.

Come on, now. Settle down and just play. Forget the audience.

She didn't. Or couldn't. She struggled all the way through the first movement. The second was not much better. Technically, she was flawless. She didn't hit one wrong note. But the flatness remained. The delicate beauty of her composition was all but lost in her lifeless performance.

The musical equivalent of someone reading the Cincinnati phone book.

The third movement, the Vivace, slowly started to come to life as she neared the end. She seemed, finally, to hit her stride. By the time she finished the long, cascading run at the end, he was sure he heard faint glimmers of the confidence he'd heard the first time she'd played it for him.

She held the last chord for several seconds, keeping the sostenuto pedal pressed. Then she lifted her foot from the pedal and let her hands drop from the keyboard.

The audience broke into applause, moderate at first, then gaining intensity. A few people stood, followed by a few more, then a few more, until all were standing.

That's incredible! Sure, her composition is wonderful, but they had to have heard how stiff and lifeless she sounded.

She stood, faced the audience, and gave an awkward bow.

Maybe they did. And maybe they either knew or sensed why. This was a brave performance, and it's possible they felt it on a gut level. Lifeless as it was, it was still amazing that she was able to get through it at all.

She finished her bow, half-ran off the stage, and collapsed into his arms.

"I stunk," she sobbed into his shoulder.

"No, you didn't," he told her. "The audience seems to feel otherwise."

"They don't know," she sobbed again.

"Yes, they do. Yes, they do. They're still applauding. Go take another bow."

He wiped the tears from her eyes and half-forced her back on the stage. She bowed again. Then she was joined by the other composers. All four joined hands and bowed in unison.

She snuggled close to him.

"Be honest. How did I really do tonight?"

He stroked her shoulder and said, "Much better than you think. You started out sounding stiff and careful. But you warmed up by the end. The point isn't how well you played it. What matters is that you hauled your quite attractive behind out onto the stage and played your piece all the way through. Given how much you fear and loathe performing, that's pretty damn impressive."

He felt her grin.

"I couldn't have done it without you."

"Sure you could. Matter of fact, you DID. If I recall, I didn't play one single note. You played all of them by yourself."

"You helped."

"I stood off to the side and watched. My Uncle Max has a word for people like that. They're called 'Supervisors.' They're the people who stand around and watch everybody else do the real work."

She giggled.

"Well, you certainly did a masterful job of supervising tonight."

"Meost kind uf you," he replied in a faux-British accent. "I'm quite humbled, eck-chewally."

She giggled again and gave his arm a playful slap.

"I mean it, though," she said. "Thanks for everything."

"Glad to help. Worth every moment, just for the chance to see you in that gown."

"I felt silly."

"You didn't look silly. The average guy would give you a standing ovation if you played 'Chopsticks.'"

She sat up, rolled her eyes and said, "Nice to know they appreciate my talent."

"We're so sensitive."

Audrey stuck out her tongue at him, but he saw merriment in her eyes.

"Well, as long as you're in such a jolly mood," he said, "mind if I ask a favor?"

"Sure."

"My senior recital's coming up. I've been working with Doc Deegan on the program. Any chance I could include your sonata?"

She paused, her body tensing.

"Umm … I don't know. Can you do that? Play a student's work?"

"Don't see why not. I played it for Deegan, and he liked it."

"Well … okay, I guess."

"Great! Can't wait to acknowledge you at the end."

"Oh, NO! I can't! I'd hide under the seats!"

"Come on," he said. "It's standard. The composer always gets a hand from the performer."

"I don't … what if the audience doesn't like it?"

"They'll like it just fine. And they'll like it even more if you wear your gown again."

"Oh, NO!" She buried her head in the pillow.

VII

Program

Three Rag-Caprices for Piano	Darius Milhaud (1892-1974)
Nocturne, Op.9, No. 2	Frederick Chopin (1810-1849)
Suite – Pour Le Piano	Claude Debussy (1862-1918)
Piano Sonata in C-Minor	Audrey Quigley (1966 –)
In A Mist	Leon Beiderbecke (1903-1931)

Intermission

Piano Concerto in F-Major	George Gershwin (1898-1937)

"Check this out," he said as he handed the program to her. "According to the program, you're actually alive!"

She responded with another of her high-strung giggles. The two of them stood, once again, in the room behind the stage.

"Look, that's very significant," he said. "I, for one, am very glad you're alive. It's one of your most attractive features."

"How can you be so relaxed? It's not even my recital, and I'm a total wreck."

"You don't look like a wreck," he told her. "Not in that outfit."

Per his suggestion, she again wore her green gown, and was again coiffed and made-up to the nines.

"Thanks," she said. "I like the way you look, too."

He wore his tuxedo, the full "penguin outfit," with black bow tie, stiff collar, and patent leather shoes.

"Don't ever again try to tell me men aren't beautiful," she said. "I can't take my eyes off of you."

"Thanks. You obviously have very good taste."

She gave him an affectionate gap-toothed smile and said, "Sounds like the old colossal monstrous ego is at it again."

"Mm-hmm," he replied with a grin.

"Oh, THERE you are," said a familiar voice. He turned to the doorway and found his sister.

"Hey, there," he said. "You're just in time."

The two of them hugged, and he said to her, "Remember my friend who needed an evening gown?"

"Sure do," his sister replied. Turning to Audrey, she said, "Good HEAVENS, you look lovely!"

Audrey blushed and lowered her gaze.

"Thank you," she murmured.

He introduced them, and the two shook hands. Then Audrey said, "I'll let you two talk. I'll be outside in the wings."

"See you there," he told her.

After she left, his sister asked, "How long have you two been an item?"

Stunned, he said, "How did you know?"

She rolled her eyes and said with a laugh, "It's obvious."

"You're the only one who's guessed."

"Don't be so sure." Dropping the playful tone from her voice, she said, "Dad sends his best."

"Thanks," he replied. "Where is he again?"

"Chile. Santiago. Big bridge project."

"How's Mom?"

"She has her good days and bad days."

"Well … I'm glad you made it."

She patted his shoulder.

"Wouldn't have missed it."

He rolled through the first three pieces. Growing up, he'd read about Dave Brubeck studying with Darius Milhaud, and immediately tracked down as many Milhaud pieces as he could. "Three Rag-Caprices" was fun, the jaunty rhythms coupled with crackling modern harmonies.

Chopin's "Nocturne" was an old friend from high school, although it took him years before he finally figured out how to play it — or more precisely, how NOT to play it. Now, he found himself fighting the urge to blush. Just one week prior, he and Audrey had one of their most memorable sessions yet, making love again and again while his "Arthur Rubenstein Plays Chopin" LP spun on his turntable.

He turned in what he thought was a pretty good version of the Debussy, and thought again how difficult it was to play it well. *You can't get away with just playing the notes! You have to do something with them, something subtle and not gimmicky.*

Then came Audrey's Sonata. The first movement, the *Allegro,* flowed easily enough, but he knew he still couldn't match her effortless gliding. He played the second moment, the *Andante,* with all the tenderness he could bring.

He tore into the third movement, the *Vivace,* with as much force and energy as he could muster. He disappeared into a trance-like state, unaware of the recital hall, the audience, even his own body. He didn't think or feel anything except the music that flowed out of his fingers, into the keys, and up out of the piano.

He finished, gradually came out of his trance, and lowered his hands from the keys. He heard the initial burst of applause, which grew in loudness and intensity. He stood, faced the audience, most of whom he could not see due to the stage lights, straightened his back, sighed, and bowed. In the front row he saw his sister standing and applauding.

The applause grew. He held out his right hand in the direction of the stage wing. Audrey carefully walked on stage. When the audience saw her, and realized who she was, they burst into an even louder crash of applause. She blushed, her face turning a shade of red almost as deep as her hair. She bowed to the audience, then faced him and applauded. He bowed to her, then held out his hand to her. They joined hands and bowed in unison. Then he impulsively hugged her and kissed her cheek. Several people in the audience responded with cheering and more applause. Audrey blushed again.

She returned to the wings, and he launched into the first half's final piece, Bix's "In A Mist." He felt supremely confident, and gave a crisp, energetic performance. In one way, he felt the same way about Bix as he did about Audrey – both of them deserved to be heard. Bix died in 1931, yet was only now starting to be taken seriously as a composer. Audrey was just getting underway, but was every bit as deserving.

He received another loud round of applause, bowed, and walked off the stage. Once backstage, he changed both his white tuxedo shirt and his undershirt. That was a lesson he'd learned during his freshman year recital. By the time he'd finished that performance, he resembled a penguin sweating like a pig. And he remembered one more hard-earned lesson – he visited the restroom and urinated copiously. He never forgot his sophomore recital when he performed Beethoven's "Pathetique" Sonata with an alarmingly expanding bladder. He'd finished and barely made it off the stage and to the men's room in time.

After intermission, the orchestra filed onstage for the Gershwin. Most piano recitals were solo, with an occasional trio piece or two. This night was different. Professor Gilman, the head of the orchestra, knew the Gershwin was every bit as much of a workout for the orchestra as for the pianist, and told everyone in the ensemble they'd be a part of this recital.

Once the orchestra was in place and tuned up, he and Professor Gilman walked onto the stage to another round of applause. He remembered to shake hands with Melanie, the principal violinist/concertmistress.

He took his place at the piano and listened as the orchestra kicked off the first movement, all pounding and crashing percussion, angular French horn riffs, and happily skipping strings.

He began the piano solo down in the lower register. Soon he was back in his trance, oblivious to everything except the music, that great Gershwin music that allowed every pianist to live and breathe, to growl in anger and shout with joy. He and the orchestra roared through the first movement and brooded through the second.

The third movement was his favorite. It kicked off with single-note staccato bursts, the sound of heavy-duty riveting, the sound you heard in New York during the twenties as workmen built bridges, skyscrapers, and battleships. He and the orchestra soared together with the angular, ascending chords. His pulse pounded as he hurtled toward the finish line with rising and falling block chords. Gilman gave the orchestra the cutoff, and the audience rose and cheered.

He let out a deep breath, stood on shaking legs, and bowed. Then, following protocol, and with his pulse still pounding, he shook hands with Professor Gilman and Melanie, and bowed to the orchestra. Gilman acknowledged Terry, the trumpet soloist, and the percussion section. He applauded all of them, shared another bow with Professor Gilman, and left the stage. He returned for two more curtain calls.

As was the case with most other recitals, a nearby rehearsal hall functioned as a reception room. Doc Deegan's wife mixed up her specialty punch that had just the right amount of tanginess to it, an almost alcohol-like edge.

He stood, back straight, still in his "penguin outfit," greeting his friends and other audience members. He congratulated Terry the trumpeter for his fine solo work, and thanked his friend Alex, the percussion section principal.

Doc Deegan, the top of his bald head shining, introduced him to Haynes D'Arcineau, the longtime music critic for the Cincinnati Enquirer. The pianist was astonished. A critic of D'Arcineau's stature rarely, if ever, attended something as lowly as a student recital. The famous critic told him, "Professor Deegan told me I'd hear something extraordinary tonight. I certainly was not disappointed."

"Most kind of you," he replied. "We're so glad you could join us."

"I was quite impressed to see you included the Beiderbecke piece. My father in law grew up with Bix in Davenport. Always good to hear his piano work performed."

"Thank you, sir. It's an honor to play Bix's work."

"I enjoyed your performance very much. Good to meet you."

"Good to meet you, too."

A few moments later, he saw D'Arcineau chatting with Audrey. She didn't have a formal reception line, but was instead mobbed by people who wanted to congratulate her and chat with her. At first, she appeared quite astonished by the attention. As she chatted with D'Arcineau, her eyes widened, and both her face and her gestures seemed to become more animated.

He turned his attention back to his line of well-wishers and accepted their congratulations with what he hoped was the proper amount of modesty and grace. As the line finally started to shorten, he glanced again at Audrey, and saw she was now hunched forward, just as she was before her recital, looking tense and wary. A few moments later, she vanished.

After the reception ended, he and his sister helped Doc Deegan and his wife clean up. He said good night to his sister and walked out into the hallway. He found Audrey, still in her gown, waiting for him.

"Hey, there," he said. "Where'd you go?"

She shook her head.

"I had to get out of there. It was fun at first. The music critic was very nice to me. But some of the people just seemed … I don't know … like they wanted something from me."

"Like you owe them something."

She nodded and said, "Yeah. Still not sure how it all feels."

"Well, listen," he said, trying to lighten the mood. "What do you say we get out of these monkey suits and go hear some jazz. A friend of mine plays at Leary's."

Her eyes widened.

"I don't know. Is it a restaurant?"

"No. Just a bar. But you don't have to order any booze. Stick with soda and listen to the music."

"Well … okay."

He grinned and added, "No one will *want* anything from you."

He drove her back to her dorm room and waited while she changed. After a brief stop at his place, where he changed out of the tux, they headed to Leary's in downtown Cincinnati.

They walked down the stairs into the crowded, smoke-filled bar. He found his friend Tony, a middle-aged black jazz trumpeter and leader of the house band.

"My man!" Tony shouted. "Heard you tore the place UP at your recital!"

"I was okay. Didn't embarrass myself too badly. This is Audrey. I played one of her compositions tonight."

"That right?" Tony grinned and shook her hand. "Love to hear it sometime."

She lowered her eyes and said, "Thank you."

Looking back at him, Tony said, "Want to sit in tonight?"

"If it's okay."

"Sure it is. We'll be getting started in just a minute."

"Sounds great."

He led Audrey to a table, ordered a seven-and-seven for himself and a club soda for her. She sat at the table, hunched forward, eyes slightly squinting.

Tony took the mike, and announced, "Ladies and gentleman, we have a special treat tonight. The star pianist of the Cincinnati Conservatory just joined us, and I've invited him to sit in. Give this man a big welcome!"

He walked onto the stage to a round of applause and took his place at the piano. Along with Tony the leader, three other black men occupied the stage – a guitarist, a bassist, and a drummer.

"Joy Spring in F?" Tony asked.

"Joy Spring in F," he answered.

They swung into the Clifford Brown tune, and he thought once again how playing jazz is damn near more fun than the law allows. *It's especially great when you play with guys like these – solid, experienced pros who've been in the business for years.*

They played one more tune, "In Walked Bud," then said to Tony, "Thanks, but I really should get back to my table and my companion." He left the stage to another round of applause and rejoined Audrey at their table. She seemed to be squinting even harder.

"Man, that was fun!" he said.

"I can tell," she replied. "Listen, I'm sorry to be a party-pooper, but could you take me home? I'm not feeling well. You can just drop me off and come back here."

"I'm so sorry," he said. "What's wrong?"

"I have a terrible headache."

Out in the car, she said, "I'm really sorry. All that cigarette smoke, the noise, the place was so crowded – I just couldn't handle it."

"It's all right," he told her. "My fault. I should have known better."

They drove back to her dorm room in silence. He pulled into the parking lot and leaned over to kiss her goodnight. Her kiss felt awfully limp and lifeless.

"Hope you feel better," he said.

"Thanks."

"See you Saturday?"

"Sure."

The Saturday morning brought blue skies filled with lovely white clouds. The April temperatures hovered in the mid-sixties. The past winter's snow and ice were long gone. His mood matched the cheery weather as he pulled into her dorm's parking lot. Within a few moments he saw her approaching. He opened the passenger door and held it open for her.

She got in, and he leaned over to kiss her. She kissed back, but once again it felt limp and lifeless.

"Feeling better?" he asked.

"Thanks. A little."

He started to put the Toyota in gear when she stopped him.

"Wait," she said in a hoarse voice. "We need to talk."

"Okay," he said, shifting into Park.

She turned her face to him. He noticed her eyes were bloodshot, and her eyelids were red around the rims.

"I'm sorry," she said. "Please don't be mad at me. I can't do this anymore."

"You ... can't?"

"No. You said I could back out anytime."

"Yeah. I'm sorry, did I do something wrong?

"No, nothing wrong. That's the problem. Remember you told me about the British guys who were sometime lovers and lifelong friends?"

He nodded.

"At first, I thought I could handle that. But as we spent more time together, I started getting depressed, knowing it wouldn't last, that it would end someday. I didn't want it to be just 'sometimes.' I needed more. Maybe I should have stopped it earlier, but it just felt so good. Remember the time I couldn't see you, couldn't face leaving my dorm room?"

"Yeah."

"It all got to me that week. How good everything was between us. And I just got so depressed, knowing I was going to lose this. But then I thought maybe we *could* make a long-term go of it. Maybe after you finish in Boston and I finish here, we could be together."

She paused and said, "The night of your recital, I realized that could never happen. All you want out of life – living in big cities, working in the studios, playing jazz, maybe even touring the world, performing with symphonies – and I can't be a part of any of that. Much as I care about you, I wouldn't be able to handle any of it. I can't be what you need."

He sighed, too stunned to say anything. Finally, he whispered, "We still friends?"

She nodded again, not meeting his gaze.

"We'll always be friends," he told her. "You'll never lose that."

"I think the world of you," she said.

"I think the world of you, too. Thanks for everything. It was great."

"It was. Thank you, too."

She opened the door, got out, shut the door behind her, and walked back to her dorm without a backward glance.

He turned off the ignition and sat in silence. He couldn't understand why he didn't try to change her mind. At last, he realized he didn't argue … because he knew she was right. She wanted more than just Sometimes. He couldn't give her more than that. And neither could she. He'd tried to help her deal with her fears, and she seemed to make some progress. But apparently not. Or at least, not enough.

She said she can't be what you need. And the reverse is true. You can't be what she needs. Audrey needs someone who will devote his whole life to her, someone who …

actually, is more like a wife. The old-fashioned definition of a wife, a woman whose whole existence revolved around her husband. Finding a man like that would be nothing short of a miracle.

Barring that miracle, she'll always have that fear of big cities, along with many other hangups. She'll probably get a job teaching at a small-town college and spend most of her time on campus, rarely straying beyond the safety of the campus borders. No doubt she will create some great music. And hardly anyone will ever hear it. And that will be a damn shame.

Over the final few weeks of his senior year, he and Audrey had passed each other quite often in the hallways. They remained polite to each other, yet he could tell she was keeping her distance. She seemed fearful of allowing herself to once again come too close.

The following year, he headed off to Berklee, up in Boston, just as planned. He wrote her several letters, but she answered only a few. When he returned to Cincinnati during the holidays, he usually phoned her. Again, she answered a few of his calls, but not all.

Near the end of his year at Berklee, he found an unexpected letter from her. She said she was finishing up her MA, and already had a job nailed down – teaching piano and theory at a private women's college in rural Ohio. He wrote back and congratulated her. She didn't answer.

PART THREE

The San Fernando Valley

VIII

H is watch beeped him awake. He slowly came out of a deep sleep, then panicked. All was dark. He sat bolt upright.

What the hell … where am I?

Then he remembered.

Casa del Crescendo.

He fumbled in the dark until he found the battery-powered lamp and switched it on. Warm welcoming light flooded the interior of his new home.

Whew! This might take a little getting used to! He thought back to the morning, four years ago, when Audrey also sat bolt upright, unsure of where she was.

He crawled out of the sleeping bag, half-stood, and opened the door. The first faint blue light of dawn lit the bushes on the hillside in front of the shed, barely edging out the yellow glow of the streetlights. The rain had stopped, but the bushes still glistened.

Day One in Casa del Crescendo.

He dressed in jeans, a red polo shirt and a blue windbreaker. As he stepped out of the door, he felt his sneakers sink into the mud. Cold water spilled off the tarp.

Ugh. This is not good. Need to get some boots. Work boots. Should have gotten them weeks ago. The hard hat and vest are convincing, but those sneakers should have given you away the moment you set up shop here.

Okay, so where to? A shoe store, a hardware store?

Try the Northridge Goodwill first. You might get lucky and find a pair at a decent price.

Umbrella in one hand, canvas sack in the other, and with the hard hat and vest in place, he squished his way through the mud, down to the gate.

He'd seen the Goodwill store several times, in a small strip mall just off the freeway. The Goodwill sat next to a McDonald's. While he waited for the Goodwill's opening hour of 8:00 AM, he allowed himself the luxury of an Egg McMuffin breakfast, and thought of the hot dogs awaiting him back at Casa del Crescendo.

They'll be dinner tonight. Let's pick up some ketchup and mustard from a Vons on the way back.

No, wait. Just get some packets from McDonald's. If not, there are other places that will have them.

Just after eight, he entered the Goodwill and headed straight for the shoe section. He searched, in vain, for a pair of size nine work boots. Nothing. All the available boots were too big or too small, and pretty ratty-looking.

Worth a shot. Long as we're here, let's look around and see if they have anything useful.

In the tool section he found several hammers, saws, and files, none of which he needed. Against the back wall stood several electric weed trimmers, which he also couldn't use. But next to the weed whackers he found a curved blade attached to a four-foot wooden handle.

A scythe! Just the ticket to keep the weeds trimmed. Let them get too long, and the Caltrans crews will come in to trim them and find everything. They'd boot you out in a heartbeat. Keep the weeds trimmed, and maybe ... maybe ... the crews just move on to the other places that need maintenance.

Yeah, but you're taking a chance. What if your old buddy Herman or one of his guys sees you trimming the weeds? They'll know right away you're not one of them. Even if they don't see you, they'll know someone other than them is doing the job.

It's worth the risk. Any luck, Herman and his guys will be glad someone is doing their work for them and will look the other way. They might even chalk it up to that contractor song and dance you told the CHP.

He picked up the scythe and moved on to the electronics section, and spotted a good-sized boom box, gray with a black face. The box came with AM and FM radio and a cassette player/recorder. The price was just five dollars.

He wasn't surprised. Ever since compact disks came out, both vinyl records and cassettes – and the equipment that played them – had plummeted in value. A few die-hards still hung on to their LPs, but cassettes were as obsolete as Thomas Edison's tinfoil cylinders.

He plugged the power cord into a wall outlet, extended the antenna, and turned the radio on. Both AM and FM came through loud and clear. He glanced around and found a section for used CDs, LPs, and cassettes. Among them, he found a cassette of "Dave Brubeck's Greatest Hits." He took the cassette over to the boom box, inserted it and pressed PLAY. A moment later the familiar strains of "Take Five" streamed through the speakers.

It works!

He checked the price of the cassette. Twenty-five cents.

A quarter! You've got to be kidding me!

He returned to the used records section and learned all the cassettes cost a quarter apiece. Scanning the bin, he found several "old friends" — cassette versions of LPs he'd once owned. "Kind of Blue" and "Miles Ahead" by Miles Davis. "Django" by the Modern Jazz Quartet. "Bernstein Conducts Bernstein," featuring "Symphonic Dances from West Side Story." "Songs for Distingue Lovers" by Billie Holliday. Holst's "The Planets," with Eugene Ormandy and the Philadelphia Orchestra.

He bought all of them and several more. He couldn't wait to get back to the shed to listen to them. It had been so long since he'd had the luxury of listening to music in private. When he moved from the two-bedroom apartment to the studio, he sent his collection of LPs and CDs back home to his sister. Now he had both a cassette player and several cassettes, all for practically nothing. All because the march of technology rendered them worthless.

Well, they're not worthless to me!

That evening, he reflected on the day's accomplishments. He found a pair of affordable boots at a nearby shoe store. He took the scythe over to the hardware store for sharpening. While waiting, he found plastic picnic chairs on sale for only a couple of bucks and indulged himself by buying one. Over at the Rite-Aid, he picked up a pair of cheap headphones, a box of trash bags, batteries for the boom box, a bottle of rubbing alcohol, and some Q-Tips. Then he stopped by a burger stand called "Rocket Burger," ordered an iced tea, and surreptitiously stuffed several ketchup and mustard packets into his pockets.

He spent the afternoon mounting the overhanging portion of the roof tarpaulin on two five-foot lumber beams. Both of the beams fit neatly into two cinderblocks. He formed a "front porch" of sorts by laying other cinderblocks, wall side up, in rows between the beams and the shed. He created a cinderblock pad for the stove out of nine of the remaining blocks, three rows of three. Then he pitched the pup tent and stored the cooler and the water jug inside.

He finished all these tasks before evening and fired up the stove for the first time. It was a tiny unit – a flat grate and burner on top of a six-inch circular tank, with a pump on one side and a regulator knob on the other. After filling it with fuel, he pumped it up, heard the hiss, struck the sparker, and saw the lovely sight of a blue flame roaring to life.

Fifteen minutes later he sat on his new plastic chair, on his "front porch," and enjoyed his first home-cooked meal: Two hot dogs with ketchup and mustard, with a side of canned corn niblets, all served in one of the scout mess kit pans with the detachable handle. Not much of a meal, but he permitted himself a small measure of pride in it.

He thought back to his time in the Boy Scouts, and how his scoutmaster taught him and his fellow scouts how to use the Coleman stove. After just a few lessons, all of the scouts in his troop became adept at camp cooking.

For some time, it's been fashionable to denigrate a man by calling him a "Boy Scout." It's supposed to infer he's a woefully naïve, hopelessly un-hip goody two-shoes. Hell, I learned to set up camp and to use this stove because of what I learned as a scout. Someone wants to call me a "Boy Scout," that's fine with me. Let's see how long they last trying to survive outdoors.

After cleaning the pans, he stored the stove in its metal container, stowed it and the can of stove fuel in the tent, and got to work on the boom box. He used the alcohol and the Q-Tips to clean the cassette player's heads, capstans, and the edges of the inside cover. After snapping the batteries in place, he inserted the headphone jack and popped the Dave Brubeck cassette into place.

"Take Five." "I'm In a Dancing Mood." "In Your Own Sweet Way." "Camptown Races." "The Duke."

All old friends. His Uncle Max bought him the LP when he was six, shortly after the piano lessons started. He listened to the album so much he wore it out and had to get a new copy in high school. One of his proudest moments came when his piano teacher gave him the sheet music to "Blue Rondo A La Turk" when he was just fifteen. Within a few months, he played it flawlessly.

He finished listening to Side B, with "Mr. Broadway" ending on its dramatic flourish. He half-stood, removed the headphones, and opened the door. The sun had set, and the last of the blue was fading from the sky. Off to his right, he heard a rustling in the weeds next to the freeway.

He froze and listened with his ear cocked. The rustling continued.

What is it? A rat, or a squirrel? A cop, or maybe another homeless guy?

He didn't make a sound. Critters would have a tough time making it into the space, as they'd have to cross either a busy street or an on-ramp. Difficult, but not impossible. Other homeless guys were more likely. If they saw him coming and going, even with the hard hat and vest, they still might guess what was up, especially if they smelled the cooking. Cops were always a threat.

He stood still for a good five minutes, listening. He heard nothing more, but felt an increasing need to pee. He thought of one more thing he'd learned in the scouts. Animals often marked their territory by urinating at the corners.

Why not follow suit? If the rustling sound was the work of a critter, it would get the message. Who knows, maybe other homeless guys would get it, too.

Using his keychain flashlight, he walked over to each darkened corner and let fly.

Yeesh. From listening to Brubeck to peeing like an animal. How the mighty have fallen. Let's hit the sack.

He sat in the laundromat and worked on a letter to his sister. Once again, he thought how lucky he was to find the laundromat just up the street from Casa del Crescendo, right next to the Denny's. His "wardrobe" was limited – underwear and socks, jeans and polo shirts. He left the cleaning of his tux, black suit, and dress shirts to the dry cleaners. Like his gym membership, the laundromat served to hide his homelessness. He made sure he set aside enough money to keep his clothes clean.

He told his sister about the film score gig with Ed, the disaster with Chuckie Betts, and the auditions with Marty Morris. He didn't say a word about Casa del Crescendo.

He'd never told her about giving up the studio apartment and moving into his car. The embarrassment was too great. Besides, he'd been so certain he wouldn't spend too much time living in the Ford. She sent her letters to his PO box after he told her about a rash of mail thefts in his old neighborhood. The mail thefts were true enough, but he hoped she hadn't guessed the real reason.

He offered his concern over the roof, and said he would try to help with the cost if he could. That was the longest of long shots. If he were still living in Casa del Crescendo next year, there would be no way he could contribute to a new roof.

He thought again of how lucky they were to even own the home. Seven years ago, their mother developed Alzheimer's. She had to be put into a specialized care home for dementia patients. His father's company health plan covered some of the cost, but not nearly enough. Soon, the costs began eating into the father's life savings.

The boat was the first to go. Then the Pontiac. The sale of both caused a sea-change in his father. He seemed to view the loss as a form of penance, the just punishment for his years of distance as both a husband and father. The gifts of the cell phones came across as awkward attempts to heal the rift between father and son.

The pianist tried to forgive, to accept the father's awkward olive branches. The two men slowly gained an aloof, polite acceptance of each other. It wasn't much, and he doubted he could ever fully forgive his father. But their tenuous bond was a start, a step in the right direction.

Not long after his mother died, his father was diagnosed with Stage Three liver cancer. The treatments threatened to eat up almost all of the remaining life savings. The sale of the house appeared to be the only remaining option.

One day, while he still lived in his apartment, his pager buzzed. The number was his sister's. He called, and she said, "It's Dad."

"What?"

"Dad. He died."

"What? When?"

"This afternoon. I was driving him home from his chemo session. He started to say something, then grabbed his chest and rolled over to the window. I drove him back to the hospital. He was dead by the time I got him there."

"Damn."

"Can you make it home for the funeral?"

"I don't know."

"I can loan you the money."

"Thanks. Let me think things through."

"Okay."

He decided to pass on his father's funeral. *Too much to do out here in LA,* he told his sister and himself. After a few weeks, he had to admit he felt relieved by his father's death. But he felt something else, something it took months for him to define. He felt a sense of mourning, not so much for his father, but for the father-son relationship they never had, the relationship that had only just started to awkwardly explore, one that now had no chance of ever developing into something resembling maturity.

The house became the property of both son and daughter. The pianist still carried mixed feelings about the house. He was happy to escape it, the place of hostility between husband and wife and father and son. He never wanted to live there again. But legally, he owned half of it. His father's early death provided his sister with a place to live, and – although he hated to acknowledge it – provided him with a back-up plan in the event he had to face up to defeat in LA and return home.

I'm not there yet. Maybe I'm living in a glorified dog house, but I'm still not ready to give up.

With his laundry finished, he drove over to the union. Once inside the lobby, he thought about calling Marty Morris to check on the status of the musical. If nothing else, the sight of him calling someone on his cell phone in the middle of the checkerboard-floor lobby made for a good visual. Just as he was getting ready to call, he saw Clarence Clendennon stride into the lobby.

Clarence was the Vice-President of the union. Tall, black, big-boned, and bald, he was the last person in the world anyone would guess to be a violist. He looked more like a linebacker. But everyone knew he was both a superb violist and someone who always had his ear to the ground.

"Morning, Clarence. How are you today?"

"Fine, fine. How are you, young man?"

Chances are, Clarence didn't know his name, even though they'd spoken several times. The Vice-President couldn't possibly be expected to know the name of everyone in the union, although he came damn close to doing just that.

"I'm well, thanks."

"Getting' any gigs?" Clarence asked.

"Some," he replied. "Worked for Marty Morris last week. Audition pianist for his new show."

Clarence's expression turned somber.

"Oh, man. Hate to tell you this, but if you were counting on that for future gigs, you're out of luck. I just heard this morning … Marty's financing fell through."

"Oh," he replied, trying to keep an impassive face and voice. "That's too bad. Tough break for Marty."

"Yeah, sure is," Clarence replied. "Tough break for a lot of folks. But you keep on pluggin,' okay?"

"Sure will."

Clarence patted his right arm and said, "I'll let you know if I hear of anything."

"Thanks."

DAMN IT!

IX

R ight to LEFT. Right to LEFT.
He swung the scythe in a 2/4 rhythm.
Almost like swinging a golf club.
Right to LEFT. Right to LEFT.

The scythe sliced through the on-ramp weeds. The dry weeds crackled with every swing.

Keep swinging this on a daily basis, and we'll qualify for the PGA Tour in no time.

The predawn sky remained a medium blue. The sun wasn't scheduled to rise for another fifteen minutes. He knew this was the best time of day for this sort of work. Early enough so that any commuters who saw him would simply think he was a Caltrans maintenance man doing his job. But he was up and about long before any actual Caltrans maintenance crew. They were not usually on site before 7:15 or 7:30. This much he had gleaned from his conversation with Herman, the Caltrans maintenance supervisor, on the morning he loaded the flakeboard into the Ford's truck bed.

Right to LEFT.

That first rainfall, just as he'd finished Casa del Crescendo, proved to be more of a tease than anything else. The winter months were supposed to be the rainy season, the time when Los Angeles received the rainwater it needed to keep from drying out. The first rainfall brought some water, but not enough. The entire LA basin now sat parched and in dire need of more rain.

He set the scythe down and picked up a rake.

BACK and forth. BACK and forth.

He pushed and pulled the rake, gathering the sliced weeds into a pile.

His gigs mirrored the drought. They started with such promise, those two days accompanying the singer/actors auditioning for Marty Morris. And just as quickly, Marty lost his financial backers. After that ... nothing. Not a damn thing.

He did all he could. He checked in to the union every day, and chatted up every band leader, every music contractor, every friend, every friend of a friend he could find. He drove over to that other Delphic Oracle of the music business, the Tower Records store on Sunset, to see what was going on, or what might be going on. The Tower's bulletin board served as an unofficial musician's newspaper. Plenty of high-profile musicians spent quite a bit of time in the store. Album-release parties and performances were common.

Nothing. Not a damn thing.

He thought about taking a temp job. He'd done it twice before. The first time, he spent six weeks wrapping palettes in a warehouse. The second job was better, a data-entry gig. Both brought in some much-needed cash. But he later learned the second temp job had caused him to miss out on a couple of high-paying recording gigs. Since then, he'd been reluctant to run the risk of losing more opportunities to jobs that were only temporary.

He regularly collected the litter from around Casa del Crescendo. He separated the cans and bottles, and ran them down to a nearby recycling center, netting a couple of bucks for his efforts. Then he tossed the plastic bags full of litter and weeds into the bed of the Ford, and tossed the bags into the first open dumpster he could find.

On most mornings, he fired up the Coleman stove and cooked a breakfast of fried eggs and thin-sliced ham. Every evening, he heated a dinner of canned chile, or spaghetti and meatballs, or New England clam chowder, or hot dogs and corn niblets. He tried to include occasional fresh fruits and vegetables in his diet, and thought that Audrey would approve of his efforts, even if his diet was far from anything that could be described as "vegetarian." But fresh fruits and vegetables were perishable, and also gave off scents that could attract critters. Canned foods were a better bet.

He had little else to do. He learned to hate so many aspects of poverty and homelessness. The gnawing fear of his little shanty being found by the CHP. The fear of his friends and fellow musicians discovering his secret. The embarrassment and humiliation of it all, of only being able to afford the cheapest food, and seeing the discreet but knowing glances in the cashier's faces when he bought just the bare minimum of generic-label food.

He hated one more aspect, one he never expected – the boredom. He couldn't allow himself to do anything that cost money. He hadn't been to a movie in years. He didn't own a television. He'd gone to see the Reds play at Dodger Stadium once, just after he'd first moved to LA. But not since. He couldn't take in a play or a musical performance.

He spent his empty time practicing, both at the union and on his piano in the new storage unit. He discovered an almost unimaginable bargain in the form of the Durant Library in Hollywood. After his morning practice sessions at the union, he checked into the library and read the trade magazines, along with the LA Times and Newsweek. He listened to their record collection and checked out books. Often, he would take the book with him to Santa Monica Beach and read while sitting in the sun. This was LA after all, and the requisite tan had to be maintained.

At night, he retreated to Casa del Crescendo and read by the light of his battery-powered lamp. When not reading, he listened to the boom box's radio, either the jazz or the classical station, or to his cassettes, all while lying in his sleeping bag. Most of the time the music brought him comfort.

But one night, he listened to "Neptune" from Holst's "The Planets," and thought once again it must be the most beautifully creepy piece of music ever composed. As it ended, with the wordless female voices trailing off, the piece sounded – for the first time – not just creepy, but bleak and desolate, lifeless, almost a musical mirror of what his life had become. He switched off the cassette deck, sat up and tightened his hands into fists.

How much more of this?

He arrived back at Casa del Crescendo early one afternoon, after spending hours practicing at the union and chatting with Clarence. He walked up to the porch, then froze.

A large, disheveled black man stood next to his tent, eating one of his apples. He forced himself to shout, "WHAT THE HELL ARE YOU DOING HERE?"

The man glared at him with vacant-eyed hostility and snarled, "Fuck you, motherfucker."

The pianist pulled out his cell phone and shouted, "Beat it, before I call the cops!"

"You ain't callin' no PO-lice," the man drawled. "They arrest yo ass in no time!"

"No, they won't!" he shot back. "I have a right to be here. I have a permit. I'm calling the cops now. If they're not here in five minutes, I'll call an ambulance!"

The man glowered at him, threw down the apple, and again snarled, "Fuck you, motherfucker." He turned and stalked away, toward the end of the wall.

The pianist shouted after him, "Fuck YOU, you worthless piece of shit! Don't you ever set foot here again!"

The man disappeared into the weeds. The pianist stood, not saying a word, for several long moments. Then he let out a long sigh.

Damn it. I used to be so honest. Now I'm lying my ass off just to guard my territory, which consists of an illegally-built shed on government property.

He thought about the man he'd just confronted.

Chances are, I might have given him the apple – IF he'd asked. But I caught him stealing, and instead of offering an apology he just spewed dull-eyed antagonism at me. Yeah, I lied to him and was pretty damn abusive with my language. But I showed him as much respect as he showed me. Any luck, he'll believe my spiel and warn other homeless guys to stay out of here. At least I hope so.

A quick inspection the tent's contents showed only the one apple missing. For that, he felt relieved.

On the other hand – all along, my big hope has been the CHP officer believing that "contractor" horseshit and repeating it to other cops and the Caltrans guys. There's a chance the homeless guy might tell the cops about the food he found in the tent, which could very well blow the cover story all to hell.

He unlocked the front door to the shed, opened the door, turned on the light, and collapsed into his sleeping bag.

I can't do this much longer! I hate what I have to do, I hate what's happening to me. I hate this life. Hate it.

The next day, as he drove to the gym, he started to feel a grinding sensation in the Ford's front end. The Ford's brakes – never that great to begin with – now needed even more force.

This isn't good. Better get these looked at.

After his workout, he drove over to the tire store that had replaced his front tire. He watched as the mechanics mounted the Ford on the hydraulic hoist, raised it several feet, and removed the front wheels.

A half hour later, the service manager told him, "Your front brake shoes are worn out. The asbestos is almost completely gone. We'll have to special-order the shoes. No one uses them anymore, and I'm not sure how much longer they'll be available."

"Nuts," he replied. "Well, let's go ahead and order them. How long will it take?"

"About a week," the manager said. "One other option. There's a disc brake conversion kit for Falcons. May want to consider it."

"How much?"

"About three hundred."

"Can't swing that just now. Maybe later."

"Okay. But I'd recommend leaving your car here. The shoes are too far gone to drive safely."

"Right. I'll need to fetch my bag."

He stood on the sidewalk, contemplating his next moves.

This is not good. LA is the most car-centric place in the world. No car, no work. We need a backup plan.

We can take the bus into Hollywood and LA for gigs. But buses are awfully slow. Need to allow for plenty of extra time. First order of business is getting bus route maps for the Valley and LA.

Something else: Bicycles. Remember all the bikes parts you saw dumped in the highway medians? You might be able to find one that's complete and salvageable.

Maybe. But there's no way to ride a bike from the Valley to Hollywood. Too far, too many hills.

Don't need to. Just use the bike for trips around the Valley. Do so even after you get the Ford back. Save a lot of wear and tear.

But where do we keep it? Riding in and out of Casa del Crescendo's space would be too obvious.

The storage unit. Plenty of room.

Okay, then. Right now, let's see if we can catch a bus that takes us close to the shed.

Two wide boulevards ran in parallel to the Ventura Freeway, Burbank Boulevard to the north, Ventura Boulevard to the south. LA Transit buses ran on both. Early the next morning he boarded a westbound bus, carrying his hard hat and safety glasses. He tried to remember the interchanges where he'd seen the abandoned bicycles.

The first two interchanges contained the usual detritus, including some bicycle wheels, but no complete bikes. He hit paydirt at the third interchange. After hopping the fence and pushing his way through the weeds, he found a dark blue bicycle lying on its side. He lifted the bike and dragged it over to the fence.

It looked fairly new. No rust or corrosion that he could see. He found one detail puzzling. The top frame tube held the words "Panasonic Sport 500."

I knew Panasonic makes consumer electronics, but bicycles, too?

Looking over the bike, he discovered it bore little resemblance to the Schwinn he rode as a teenager. This bike's handlebars weren't straight. Instead, the outer ends curved under. Two levers – probably brake levers – were attached to the outer ends. The pedals attached to two sprockets, one larger than the other. The rear wheel hub held five smaller sprockets.

Must be a ten-speed.

He pulled a rag from his back pocket and wiped some of the grime from the frame. Two small levers sat on either side of the steering column. Cables ran from both levers to the pedal disk and rear wheels. Shift levers, obviously. He lifted the bike, rotated the pedals and moved the shifters. The chain moved smoothly from sprocket to sprocket, even though it looked pretty dry.

Seems to work just fine. Wonder why anyone would dump a bike like this? Unless … maybe it was stolen. It happens. Someone steals something just for kicks, then dumps the item once the thrill wears off.

He finished wiping the last of the grime off the frame. Then came the hard part – lifting the bike over the five-foot-high fence and placing it on the ground without dropping it. And doing so while no one was watching. He walked the bike over to the fence and checked for cars.

Three cars passed by in succession. He was about to start lifting the bike when another car passed. Then another. Then an eighteen-wheeler.

Come on, people! Do we all have to show up right at this moment?

The cars finally disappeared. He lifted the bike up and over the fence. Then down, slowly lowering it by moving his hands gradually backward to the end of the frame, then the back end of the rear wheel. The front wheel made contact with the ground. He held the wheel against the fence with one hand and tied the rag around the rear wheel rim and the fence. After hopping over the fence he untied the rag and set the bike level on the ground. He squeezed the tires, feeling for air pressure, and was not surprised to find both were flat.

He half-carried the bike forward until he came to a cross street. Looking south, he spied a gas station a few blocks away. He continued to half-roll, half-carry the bike down the street until his arms started to protest. The gas station seemed to get farther away with each passing moment.

At last he arrived, his arms feeling leaden. He paid a quarter for the air-pump machine that quickly filled the tires.

Okay. Time to learn how to ride a ten-speed.

He mounted the bike and pedaled his way back up to Ventura Boulevard. The resistance was light – obviously low gear. He accelerated and experimented with the shifting levers until he found the right combination. He stayed on the shoulder, as far away from the traffic as he could.

Not bad! This is actually kind of fun!

He felt a rush of wind on his left ear. A delivery van with an outsized side mirror accelerated past him. The mirror probably came within a few inches of his head.

Not so fun!

He rode until he came upon the storage unit, parked the bike inside, then rode the bus to the Van Nuys public library. Inside, he found several books on riding and maintaining ten-speed bikes. He checked out two of them and returned to Casa del Crescendo.

The new brake shoes finally arrived, and the Ford was back up and running within a day. But the bill took a big bite out of his savings. Every day, he did all he could to hunt up gigs. Something, anything.

Help finally arrived in the second week of November. Clarence, the Union VP, was as good as his word and sent him a gig, a retirement party on the Queen Mary.

He arrived fifteen minutes before 5:00 PM, dressed in his black suit, and found the room set aside for the party. The room came with a Baldwin grand piano tucked in a corner. Next to the piano he found a microphone plugged into an amplifier.

Oh, hell! I hope they don't expect me to sing!

He took his place on the bench and ran through his usual warmup routine – scales, arpeggios, and a few of the Hanon exercises. Just as he finished, a sixty-something woman with blonde/gray hair, wearing a dark blue evening gown, strode up to him and said, "Oh, THANK you SO much for being here! I'm Karen. My husband is the guest of honor."

"My pleasure," he answered.

"Now be SURE to help yourself to as MUCH food as you want!" she beamed.

"Thank you."

"One other thing. My husband and I have a few favorite songs. I'd like to sing them to him. Would you be able to accompany me?"

"Be glad to," he lied. "What songs?"

"Do you know 'Day In, Day Out' and 'Crazy?'"

"Sure."

"How about 'My Funny Valentine?'"

"I know it."

He hated that tune, but tried to keep the distaste out of his voice.

"Would you like to run over all three before the guests arrive?"

She seemed a bit taken aback. The idea of rehearsing apparently had not occurred to her.

"Well … sure, why not?"

He played Floyd Cramer's slip-note intro to "Crazy," and she began singing. He was not surprised to learn she was awful. Her vocal delivery consisted of (more or less) pitched shouting. He gritted his teeth all the way through the three songs.

They finished, and she gushed, "Oh MY, that was LOVELY! You play so BEAUTIFULLY!"

"Thank you," he replied, offering what he hoped was a charming smile. "You sing very well."

"Oh, that's so SWEET of you!" she trilled. "Well, the guests are starting to arrive. You go ahead and play whatever you want."

He ran through his repertoire of jazz standards, tunes from the Great American Song Book, and even some soft rock numbers. Soon, the room filled with guests, and the combined hum of all those conversations drowned out anything he tried to do.

I could play Stravinsky and Bartok and no one would notice!

He played for about forty minutes, then took the "union break." As he walked over to the food table, he felt a tap on his shoulder. He turned and saw a blue-suited, gray-haired man who looked familiar.

"Hi," the man said. "I'm Herman. Remember? I helped you with the lumber."

He froze.

Shit! Herman, the Caltrans supervisor! Does he know …?

With the calmest voice he could muster, he told Herman, "Oh, sure. Didn't recognize you without your hard hat. Thanks again for letting me grab all that lumber. Saved me some money."

"What did you do with it?" Herman asked.

"Built a shed," he replied, truthfully enough.

"Like to see it," Herman said.

Damn it, does he know more than he's letting on?

"I have some pictures at home," he told Herman. Again, it was truthful. Changing the subject, he asked, "What brings you here tonight? Is the guest of honor a friend of yours?"

"We work together," Herman told him. "He's an engineer with Caltrans."

Oh, hell! Half the people in this room might know about me!

Herman patted his arm and said, "Well, go ahead and get something to eat. By the way, do you know the song 'Ojos Verdes?'"

"Sure. I'll play it for you first thing."

"Thanks."

The encounter with Herman bothered him the rest of the night, and all the way back to Casa del Crescendo. Herman definitely seemed to know more than he was letting on. If so, he was looking the other way, at least for the time being. But there was no telling how much longer he would be willing or able to do so, especially if a certain homeless black man told him about food in a tent.

Better step up the search for a roommate. You could get busted at any moment.

With the money from the Queen Mary gig deposited in his account, he rode down to the bike shop just next to his self-storage unit. The sign above read "Riley's Cyclery." He walked his bike into the store and found rows of shiny new bicycles, tires hanging from the ceilings, and display cases full of merchandise. Behind a glass counter stood a man with shoulder-length hair and a full beard. He wore jeans and a T-shirt. The shirt sported a stop sign, with the word "Driving" beneath the sign.

"Hello," the man said.

"Hello. You Riley?"

"That's me. Panasonic. Nice bike."

"Thanks. Sure is."

"They stopped selling them in the US couple of years ago."

"That right? Didn't know that."

"How long you've had it?"

"Just a couple of weeks. Thing is, I found it in a highway shoulder and pulled it out of the weeds. Might be stolen, but I didn't want to see it rot away."

"Let's get a look at her."

Riley spent a few minutes looking the bike over.

"Not too bad, considering," Riley said. "Brakes look okay. You'll want to get a new chain and cassette."

"A cassette?"

"The rear sprockets. They're sold as a package. Also, your tires aren't falling apart, but you'll want to replace them in a few months. One thing, though. If it is stolen, and the owner comes forward, you could be out that money."

The pianist nodded and said, "I'll take that chance."

Riley answered, "Tell you what. All the bike shops in the Valley have an unofficial list of stolen bikes. I'll run yours by them. If nothing hits, we'll go ahead with the work."

"How about the cops?"

"Nah, too many stolen bikes for them to deal with. Besides, yours is an '85. Not too many people are going to stress over an eight-year-old bike."

A few days later, with no hits coming from the stolen bike list, Riley installed the new chain and cassette. Although the pianist didn't follow Riley's T-shirted advice to "Stop Driving," he found himself driving a whole lot less. Just as he thought, cycling saved quite a bit of money, as gas prices were once again creeping upward. But it also gave him an unexpected release, a way of clearing out some of the ongoing tension, the stress of constant money worries and the fear of either the CHP or his fellow musicians discovering his secret living arrangements.

He soon learned Riley possessed the equivalent of a Ph.D. in bicycling. In addition to the maintenance and repair of bikes, Riley taught him about the preferred cycling routes across both the Valley and the LA Basin. An unrepentant sixties hippie, Riley often lectured at length on the spiritual advantages of cycling and the evils of motorized traffic. He recommended a couple of two-lane roads that crossed over the Santa Monica Mountains into Hollywood.

The pianist accepted the mountain routes as a challenge. He took the steep uphill roads in increments, until one cool sunny day he pedaled all the way to the thousand-foot-plus summit. Gazing down at the expansive view of Los Angeles, he felt a sense of triumph and renewed self-worth he hadn't experienced since arriving in LA. Even the construction of Casa del Crescendo was no match. He had to keep the shed a secret, but he could tell everyone about the mountain ride.

A few days later, as he examined the latest magazines on the rack in the library, he found one that caught his attention.

"Civil Engineering Quarterly."

He'd seen his father reading the magazine quite often when he was growing up. He'd never bothered to read it. Almost to his surprise, he pulled the magazine down from the rack and flipped through it.

On page 40, he came across an advertisement for Anson, Pawling, and Associates. His father's old outfit. They were still in business, with contracts from all over the world. The top right-hand corner of the ad featured the company's logo.

He thought for a moment.

Run this over to the copying machine. Make sure it's a color copier.

He placed the ad page on the copier. A moment later, a perfect color reproduction of the ad shot out of the tray. He picked up the sheet, borrowed a pair of scissors from the desk, and cut out the Anson Pawling logo.

Glue this to the front of your hard hat. You'll look even more official. No one would dare argue with an Anson Pawling supervisor!

In early November, Skip called and offered him another gig, a wedding reception at a private home up in Holmby Hills. Skip told him the gig came with good money, more than just union scale.

As he drove the Ford through the tree-lined streets, the excitement he felt over the prospect of a good-paying gig began to mix with a deepening unease. Holmby Hills rose well above LA proper, both geographically and economically. Massive mansions stood guard over forested acres.

He found the address on Charing Cross Road. A gate of two gray stone pillars and black wrought iron blocked all outsiders. The gate guard, a burly, blonde young man dressed in black, stopped him with a glower and a raised hand.

"I'm the pianist with the band," he told the guard.

The guard pulled out a clipboard, scanned through the names, and pressed a button on the left-hand stone pillar. The wrought iron gate groaned open. The guard waved him through. He drove forward and found a collection of parked Rolls-Royces, Ferraris, and Porsches.

What the HELL am I doing here? My little Ford is probably going to set off alarms. I will, too, if any one of the guests has the slightest inkling of where I'm living these days.

Another burly young man, this one dressed in a white shirt and black pants, guided him to a parking space in the massive driveway. An imposing, gray-stone Tudor mansion loomed in the distance. He parked the Ford and shut off the engine.

"Hi, there!" a voice called. A short, red-haired man wearing a blue blazer, gray slacks, a white silk shirt, and a red silk tie approached him and asked, "Is that a '62 Ranchero?"

"No, a '63. But a good call. Not many people recognize these."

The man laughed and said, "I own a Ferrari dealership, but can still spot a Ranchero a mile away. My old man owned one. Racked up a couple hundred thousand miles on it. He'd still have it if not for the rust. We grew up in Ohio. Rust back there is a killer."

"I know. I grew up in Cincy."

"Dayton. I'm Andy."

The pianist introduced himself and the two shook hands. Andy asked, "Are you a friend of the bride or the groom?"

"Neither. I'm part of the musical entertainment."

"Really? I play a little guitar."

"Want to sit in with us?"

Andy laughed and said, "Not a chance. Don't want to embarrass myself. Listen, follow me and I'll introduce you to Armand, the father of the bride. He's one of my customers."

Andy led him through the massive mansion until they came out to the "back yard," an enormous manicured lawn under a canopy of oak trees. To the left of a covered swimming pool, a group of workmen finished assembling a wood parquet dance floor. Several long tables with white tablecloths lined the sides of the lawn. A baby grand piano stood next to the rest of the band's setup.

"Armand, how're you doing?"

Andy greeted a tall man with salt and pepper hair who also wore a blue blazer with a white silk shirt, but sported a red ascot in lieu of a tie.

"Fine, fine," Armand said. "So *glad* you could *join* us."

"This is your pianist for the evening," Andy told him. "He's a man after my own heart. Drives my favorite car of all time, a '63 Falcon Ranchero."

Armand looked at the pianist with distaste and didn't offer his hand.

"Nice to meet you."

"Pleased to meet you, sir. I'd better get things set up with Skip. You'll excuse me."

That was normal enough. He was used to the snubs of the non-musicians who hired him. But Andy surprised him. The thirty-year old Ford was – in the eyes of a Ferrari dealer – The Belle of the Ball.

Gotta love that guy!

He found Skip, who introduced him to the other musicians. The band was, so to speak, a small big band. Piano, guitar, bass, and drums made up the rhythm section, with an ensemble of trumpet, alto sax, trombone, and baritone sax. The pianist knew some of the guys from previous gigs. They cruised through the first set, alternating songbook standards with some pop hits from the sixties and seventies.

The band finished their first set and walked over to the buffet table. Armand's wife, a short, thin woman named Margaret, told them to "help yourselves," to which Skip replied, with his best charmingly boyish grin, "You may live to regret that. We're starving musicians, after all!"

Margaret gave an elegant laugh and said, "If that's the case, then the offer goes double!"

The pianist fought the urge to pile his plate full of food. "Starving musician" jokes aside, this was the best food he'd seen since the Queen Mary gig. He could barely contain his urges. Salads, fruits, cheese, crab, shrimp, salmon, ham, roast beef …

Beats the heck out of chile and hot dogs! But take it easy, now. Don't make a spectacle of yourself.

He ate slowly, with as much dignity as he could muster, during the fifteen-minute break. When the musicians resumed their places on the small bandstand, a lovely black-haired woman wearing a dark blue bridesmaid's gown greeted him.

"I'm Payton," she said. "The bride's my sister. May I ask a favor?"

"Of course."

"I'd like to sing 'Our Love is Here to Stay' to the bride and groom. Do you know it?"

"We do. What key do you prefer?"

"F."

"Any tempo preference?"

She smiled at him, revealing perfect teeth. The unusual combination of black hair and green eyes accented her lovely features. Her eyes seemed enormous, and brought back powerful memories of Audrey.

"Medium swing."

Girl seems to know what she's doing!

Payton walked over to her father, and the two of them chatted for a moment or two. Then the father lifted his wine glass and tapped it with a fork. The crowd quieted.

"Friends and family," he said into a microphone. "I've been blessed with two beautiful daughters. Carlisle is the lovely bride. Now her sister Payton would like to sing one of her favorite songs to the newlyweds."

The father handed the mike to Payton. She glanced at the pianist and offered another enchanting smile.

"Let me give you an intro," the pianist said. "Three bars, plus the downbeat."

She nodded. He played the three bars plus the downbeat. The bassist and the drummer joined in, the drummer whooshing lightly with his brushes. Payton sang, "It's very clear … our love is here to stay …"

She's good, all right. Accompanying some singers, like the Caltrans engineer's wife at the Queen Mary gig, felt like hard labor in a Soviet gulag, as if you were dragging them through a song. But Payton reminded him of a good dance partner, easy, graceful, and effortless.

"Our love is here … to … stay …"

The bride and groom listened to Payton with warmth in their eyes. Carlisle the bride was taller than Payton, with light brown hair and the same green eyes.

Good-looking, but no match for her sister.

Payton finished to a great round of applause and bowed. Then she turned to the trio, asked them to stand and applauded them. The three of them stood and returned her applause.

Hours later, he sat at the counter in the Denny's, still wearing his black suit, sipping a cup of decaf coffee. He should have been in a better mood. He had one a hell of a good gig. The money was great, the guests loved the music, and Armand, the father of the bride, made a point of thanking them. He even shook their hands.

He kept replaying, again and again, the look Payton gave him as she applauded the trio. Those enchanting green eyes seemed filled with an intense warmth as she smiled at him. Her bridesmaid's gown did not hide her bombshell figure, not one damn bit. During one of the breaks, she came over to chat with him about music. She played piano too, and they compared notes on their favorite classical piano works. The look in her eyes first excited, then depressed him.

If she only knew. What would a Holmby Hills woman think if she found out you're living illegally in a wooden shed by a freeway? She wouldn't give you the time of day. Or even worse ... she would feel sorry for you.

He paid the check, then picked up his canvas bag and headed to the men's room. Once inside, he changed out of his suit and into his polo shirt and jeans. He carefully folded the white shirt and suit and placed them inside the canvas bag.

He left the Denny's, started the Ford, and drove down to the strip mall parking lot. Once again, he donned his hard hat, safety glasses, and orange vest, and locked the Ford. He walked along the cold sidewalk until he reached the gate to Casa del Crescendo. He unlocked the gate and pushed through the moist, redolent bushes up to the shed. As usual, he used his keychain flashlight to check for any signs of disturbance to his encampment, either by Caltrans, the CHP, or other homeless people. Seeing none, he unlocked the door, stepped inside and switched on the lamp. He slipped his suit and shirt into the garment bag that held his black shirt and tuxedo, and placed the bag underneath the sleeping bag, where the garments would stay pressed. After undressing, he climbed into the sleeping bag and switched off the lamp.

I can't do this much longer. Something has to break open for me. I can't live like this. I'm tired of hiding, of looking over my shoulder all the time. I can't ...

He placed his hands over his eyes and gritted his teeth, but it was no good. Something cracked open inside him. His eyes filled with tears and his body started to shake.

This is no way to live. I can't do this. I hate this.

Yet the days still went by with no gigs. He hustled all he could, but ran into one dead end after another. Soon, his checking account reached alarmingly low levels. His savings account was off-limits, the source of his next apartment, or even just a decent room, but he worried he might have to dip into his precious savings just to meet the daily expenses – food, gas, laundry. Even his daily bike rides couldn't reduce the gnawing unease.

The second week of December, while he read the LA Times in the library, his pager buzzed. He saw the number of Ed, the composer. He walked into the hallway, turned on his phone and called the number.

"Hi, this is Ed."

"Hello, Ed. You just paged me?"

"Sure did. I'm over at Van Brocklin's studios. How soon can you get here?"

"Right away. What's up?"

"A friend has a session today for Pacific records. His pianist just called in and said he can't make it. Can you?"

"Sure! Could you let them him know I'm on the way?"

"Will do. Have fun!"

"Thanks."

He drove the Ranchero as rapidly as he dared through the Hollywood streets and arrived at Van Brocklin's Melrose Avenue studio about fifteen minutes later. Once inside, he found a studio with dark brown wood walls and a large glass window separating the control room from the rest of the studio. He introduced himself to Maury, the producer.

"Thanks for getting here so quickly," Maury told him through a craggy smile. Short, stumpy, bespectacled and bald, Maury was a legend in LA circles, a producer who coaxed first-rate records out of marginally-talented singers. He did so by – among other things – hiring not just the best studio musicians available, but the musicians best suited for any given song.

"Glad to."

He thought about asking Maury why the regular pianist didn't show, but decided against it. Instead he asked, "What can I do for you today?"

"Do you know Tommy Hartrick?"

"Know of him."

Hartrick was an up-and-coming young singer who'd had a middling-good hit song earlier in the year.

"We're finishing up his second album. Just one song today, and just piano, bass and drums. Tommy's warming up now."

"Sounds good. Let me look the music over while he's getting ready."

He took his seat at the piano bench and scanned the sheet music. The C-Minor tune appeared to be a love song. He fiddled with the chord progressions, then fell silent when Tommy Hartrick came into the room. Hartrick settled himself into a separate booth without saying hello and placed the earphones over his head.

The song was titled, "Evermore," and was yet another ballad about falling in love with someone unobtainable, although the reasons why the other person was unobtainable never became clear. Chances are, the lyricist kept things unclear for artsy reasons. The first and second verses ended with the words, "I would/if I could/be yours/evermore."

He didn't much care for the way Tommy sang. Hartrick sounded like he was pushing things too hard, trying to sound oh-so-sensitive and soulful and vulnerable. Instead he just sounded desperate and needy.

My opinion doesn't matter. Who knows, maybe some people like that.

As they played the third verse – the bridge – he listened as Tommy sang, "I wonder … if you know … how much I feel…" The chord progressions – F-Minor 7 to E-Flat Major, then B-Flat to A-Flat – triggered something. Through the final verse, he searched his memory … then remembered.

Oh, man, that would be perfect!

They finished the first take. Maury and Tommy retreated to the control booth to listen to it.

Maybe I should run this by them!

No, dammit, you're just the hired help. Don't get above yourself!

But it's worth it. Maury will probably like it. If he does, everyone else will fall into place, that's for sure.

Maury and Tommy returned from the booth. Tommy went to use the men's room.

Here goes!

"Uh, Maury?"

"Yeah?"

"Hope I'm not out of line … but could I suggest something?"

Maury hesitated, then said, "Let's hear it."

"It's something a friend of mine wrote. Just like the bridge, it starts out F-Minor 7 to E-Flat Major. But then … it goes from F-*Seventh* to E-Flat *Minor,* with the bass moving from F to G-flat. Then back to F-Minor 7 to E-Flat, then B-Flat to A-Flat. The sudden move to E-Flat Minor gives it a feeling of, I don't know … gravitas. Or something."

Maury nodded. "Let's hear what it sounds like."

The pianist played and sang:

"I wonder … if you know …"

(F-Minor 7– E-Flat *Major*)

"I wonder … if you *know* …"

(F-Seventh – E-Flat *Minor*)

"I wonder … if you know …"

(F-Minor 7 – E-Flat Major)

"How much … I feel …"

(B-Flat Major – A-Flat Major)

Maury stayed silent and looked slightly displeased. Then he pulled out his flip phone and said, "Let me call Darren. He wrote the thing. He'll have to sign off on this."

Maury called the songwriter and held out the phone as the pianist played the progression for him. Tommy Hartrick returned from the restroom and listened to the chords. More long silence followed, along with a few *mmm-hmms* from Maury as he spoke to Darren. Then he held his phone away.

"Darren likes the sound of it. But we can't just sing the same lyric three times. We'll have to come up with something new."

Tommy said, "How about, for the second … 'I hope you don't know.'"

Maury repeated it to Darren. After a few more moments, he *mmm-hmmed* one last time, told Darren, "Thanks, man," and hung up.

"Okay," Maury said. "Darren had one more line. 'I'll never let you know.' Let's try it first. If it works, we'll lay down another take."

Tommy sang,

I wonder … if you know …

I hope … you don't know …
I'll never let you know …
How much I feel … "

They recorded another take, and the session ended with more craggy smiles from Maury. Tommy made a point of shaking the pianist's hand and thanking him. The bassist and drummer also complimented him. After the others left, Maury asked, "You say that was from a friend's song?"

"A piano sonata, actually."

Maury grinned and said, "Sounds like he's pretty good."

"*She* is."

Maury blinked.

"Oh? Where is *she* now?"

"Ohio. Teaching piano and theory at a private women's college."

"We could use her out here."

"I'll tell her."

"You still in touch with her?"

"Every now and then."

"Give me her contact info," Maury said. "We'll want to cut her a check. Just a four-bar phrase, but sure makes a difference."

"Will do. Thanks again for calling me."

Maury shook his hand and said, "I'll be in touch."

<hr>

As he drove back to Casa del Crescendo, the pianist again thought, *That Audrey. She could have been something, both as a pianist and as a composer.*

Maybe I should call her. She might be pleased to know her chord progressions made it into a pop song. Or horrified.

He checked his watch. 4:30 p.m.

Too late today. Call her tomorrow morning.

X

The following morning, he drove to the union and checked out a practice room. Settling in, he plugged in his cell phone, called information, and got the number for Audrey's Ohio college. He punched it up, and a woman's voice answered, "Good morning, Gladwyn College School of Music."

"Good morning. May I please have the extension for Audrey Quigley?"

The woman didn't answer.

"Are you there?" he prompted.

"Yes," the woman finally answered. "Were you a friend of Professor Quigley?"

"We knew each other at Cincinnati Conservatory."

"I'm … I guess you didn't hear. Ms. Quigley passed away."

He almost dropped his phone. He grasped it tightly and half-grunted, "Passed away? When?"

"Eight months ago. I'm sorry."

"How?"

"You should speak with Professor Wintermantle. They were friends. I'll transfer you."

"Thank you."

Hands shaking, he listened as the line rang twice. A charcoal-voiced woman answered, "Alice Wintermantle."

"Hello," he answered. "I'm sorry to bother you. But I knew Audrey Quigley at the Cincinnati Conservatory, and just … just found out. The woman who answered the main line said you were a friend."

"Yes, that's right," the charcoal voice replied. "I think I know who you are. You're calling from Los Angeles, right?"

"That's right."

"Audrey told me about you. Always good things. She said you gave her confidence."

"That's … good to know. How did … what caused …."

"Ovarian cancer."

"Damn it," he whispered, his voice becoming more guttural with every sentence. He felt as if he'd swallowed a massive shard of ice.

"Something I should probably tell you. Not too many people know. Audrey and I were more than just friends. We were … partners."

He choked and cleared his throat.

"Par .. partners?"

"Partners. And yes, it means just what you think."

"I … I mean … I had no idea."

She sighed and said, "Neither did she."

"How …?"

"I teach musicology. Play a little piano, too. One day, she and I were chatting in my office after classes ended. I'd been taken with her from the start, but figured her for straight. On the spur of the moment, we decided to play Shubert's Fantasia, the four-handed piece. We sat together on the piano bench and had a great time. We finished, and hugged, and then … we kissed. Next thing you know … we're at my place."

His mind reeled. He thought back to all the time he and Audrey spent in bed together, and he just couldn't …

"I'd like to visit her grave sometime," he said. "Do you know where she's buried?"

"She isn't. We scattered her ashes on a hill that overlooks the campus."

He winced and said, "She was a genius."

"She was."

"And beautiful."

"She was."

"Have you hung on to her work?"

"Yes. Once she received the diagnosis, I told her to give all of her work to me for safekeeping."

"I'm grateful. Someday, I hope to introduce her work to a wider audience."

"I'd like that."

"Well," he sighed, "I know this must be difficult for you. Thanks for letting me know."

"I'm glad you called."

He hung up the phone and sat quietly on the piano bench for several long moments.

Damn it. She was just twenty-seven years old. She deserved better.

He put his hands on the keyboard and started playing the first movement of her piano sonata. He surprised himself by remembering all of it, note for note. But he was only able to make it through the first half when he had to stop, unable to continue …

The next week, as he came out of the Hollywood post office, he found the Ford's driver's side mirror smashed. Replacing it would cost money, just about the cost of his insurance policy's deductible. The process required taking out the door panels, which required tools and materials he didn't have. He was lucky to find a garage willing to install a used mirror he found in a junkyard. Most shops would only work with new parts.

A few days after the mirror was fixed, he came down with a cold. Dealing with a cold was miserable enough when living in a house or apartment. The experience was far worse when living in an unheated wooden shed. While winters in Los Angeles were nothing like those in Cincinnati, the days were still gray and cheerless. With the temperatures dropping into the forties at night, Casa del Crescendo soon became a cold and damp place. He spent days in the shed, drinking the generic green liquid cold medicine, running through several boxes of tissues, and barely eating. His pager didn't buzz even once, which was a relief. He didn't want to have to turn down a gig because of a lousy cold.

When he recovered, he found LA to be sunny again, and in full Christmas mode. Two years in, the sight of warm, snowless Southern California wrapped in Christmas decorations still jarred him. He took bittersweet comfort in his short Christmas gift list – just his sister. While visiting a Borders one afternoon he bought a book he'd seen on the bestseller list, "Mama Makes Up Her Mind," a collection of funny stories by a woman who taught school in rural Georgia. He was pretty sure his sister would get a kick out of it.

For most musicians, Christmas means one or two paydays, and he was no exception.

He and Skip played for a couple of office holiday parties, and he played another one by himself. The gigs paid well, which was good, because most of the songs they had to play were awful. During one gig, someone asked him to play a cha-cha version of "The Little Drummer Boy." He was pretty sure everyone in Los Angeles County could hear his teeth gritting.

One week later, he and Skip were invited to perform with Ralph McCall's prestigious big band for a New Year's Eve gig at a swanky country club in Beverly Hills. McCall's was the band of choice among LA's wealthier circles. The gig paid very well, the food was great, and McCall stayed with his big band arrangements of American Song Book classics. No Christmas cha-cha.

As everyone counted down to midnight, the pianist gave himself an ultimatum:

You have four months to find a place to live. No more. If you are still living in Casa del Crescendo after four months, then pack it up and go home.

He finished his grocery shopping at the Hollywood Vons and walked out into the dark parking lot. He had parked his Ford in a corner. When he arrived, his parking space was surrounded by cars. Now the corner was deserted, save for one idling car behind his. A light rain left the parking lot glowing.

Just as he reached the Ford ... a blinding white flash filled his eyes. The back of his head exploded in pain. He stumbled forward, dropped his grocery bag, and felt a pair of rough hands shove him down, face-first, on the cold, wet asphalt. A round steel tube stabbed the skin in the back of his neck, and a hoarse voice shouted, "DON'T MOVE!"

"Uhhh," he grunted. His heart hammered as one rough hand reached into his back pocket and yanked out his wallet. The other hand kept the steel tube burrowed into his neck, while a knee dug into his lower back. His pulse hammered loudly, threatening to burst his eardrums.

"STAY DOWN AND DON'T MOVE!" the voice hissed. "DON'T LOOK AROUND! I'LL BLOW YOUR FUCKIN' HEAD OFF!"

The pressure from the steel tube and the knee lifted. He heard footsteps running toward the car behind him. Then the car screamed out of the parking lot.

The back of his head throbbed and his pulse still pounded. He got to his shaking knees, looked around, and saw no one in the lot.

No witnesses! Dammit!

He opened the car door and retrieved his phone. *At least the bastard hadn't taken that.* He called information and asked for the LA Police Department's Hollywood station.

Twenty minutes later, an officer arrived to take the report. The cop seemed bored, as if he knew damn well nothing could be done. No witnesses, no description of the assailant.

The officer asked for his address, and he gave his post office box.

"Don't you have a street address?"

His throbbing skull led to a moment of careless honesty.

"At this time, I don't have an address. I'm living … in my car."

The cop gave him a look that could only be interpreted as an expression of contempt and told him, "Well, perhaps this will motivate you to find a place to live."

The throbbing head and the condescending words were too much.

"Officer, with all due respect, that's uncalled-for. I'm not …. homeless … because I'm lazy or a drug addict. I'm homeless because I'm trying to make a living in a very demanding career field. What money I make, I make honestly. I've never taken a dime in public assistance, even though I'm legally eligible. I've never panhandled, and I've damn sure never robbed anyone. I'm a law-abiding citizen, and I think I deserve a little more respect from someone who is supposed to help crime victims."

The cop looked down and continued writing. After a few moments of silence, he tore out two pages. Without looking up, he said, "Here is your copy of my initial report. Also, a form that states your license was stolen. You'll need that to drive."

"Thank you."

The officer finally looked up, met his gaze, and said, "You'll want to get that head looked at. Could have a concussion."

"I will, thanks."

***

"Ugh," the doctor grunted.

The pianist sat in the ER with the white curtain drawn around him. The doctor stood behind his back.

"Pretty nasty," the doc said. "Are you feeling dizzy? Nauseated?"

"A little," he replied. "Hard to say. The head hurts so much, it's hard to feel anything else."

"Look, I think we should keep you overnight for observation. There's a lot we don't know about concussions. You seem okay, but it's hard to tell for sure. We'll have a better idea tomorrow morning."

"If you think so."

As he filled out the interminable paperwork, he was again grateful that he had signed up for the union's health insurance plan. It didn't cover everything, but it would handle most of this visit. A nurse took him to his room, a double. Fortunately, the other bed was empty.

The bed felt odd. It had been a long, long time since he'd spent the night in something other than a sleeping bag. The doctor prescribed a couple of pain relievers for him, but his head still throbbed. He had to sleep either on his side or his stomach. When he turned on his back, the pain stabbed him awake.

He tossed and turned, still angry about the day's events. The humiliation of the robbery left him feeling powerless and beaten. He fretted over what the robber would do with the contents of his wallet. There was the further humiliation from the cop, and the knowledge that most people would have agreed with the officer. He thought of Payton and wondered again how she would react.

Maybe I've had enough. I can take the poverty and the deprivation. I can take the loneliness. But there is only so much humiliation I can endure. Maybe it's time. Time to pack it in and head back to Ohio. Time to get a fulltime job and a place to live, where I can lead a life with some semblance of dignity. Maybe it's time, after all ...

He drifted off to sleep just after midnight.

He awoke in the darkness, just before four-thirty, and felt an urgent need to pee. He switched on the light and stumbled to the bathroom. Just as he let go, he felt and heard the floor rumble.

Brrrrmppp ...

What the hell ...?

The floor shook harder. Then he noticed the mirror quivering. The rumbling gave way to violent shaking. The entire hospital building twisted and bounced.

Holy shit! An earthquake!

Someone once told him a doorway was a safe place to stand during a quake. He stood in the bathroom doorway, bracing himself, as the flexing and rolling reached alarming levels. Finally, the shaking stopped.

Whew!

He walked down the hallway to the desk. A nurse spoke rapidly on the phone. He waited until she hung up.

"Listen," he told her, "you're going to have plenty of patients soon. I'm just here for observation. Go ahead and discharge me. I'm okay."

"Let me have a doctor look at you first. Go back to your room and wait."

He returned to his room. As he waited, he felt the beginnings of another rumble. Soon, the building twisted and bounced in an aftershock.

Ride the wild surf!

A half-hour later, after another doctor gave him a perfunctory exam, he was discharged. He walked out into the early morning sunshine in the parking lot and started the Ford. He switched on his Emerson radio and listened to the news from KNX. The anchors and reporters sounded as if they were struggling to keep the ragged emotions out of their voices. A section of the I-10 collapsed at La Cienega Boulevard. An overhead connecting ramp to the Antelope Valley freeway in the Newhall Interchange fell in a heap onto the I-5. Many buildings suffered major damage. Despite the damage, drivers still flooded the freeways.

He drove from the hospital back to Casa del Crescendo, using only surface streets. But they were nearly as crowded as the freeways. Several traffic lights either flashed red or were out completely. The quake and the aftershocks left some sections of roadway badly cracked and split. The cars had to stop and then slowly make their way over the cracks, which created massive backups..

After an eternity of creeping slowly along the streets, he reached the strip mall. He parked, then sprinted across the street. He unlocked the gate, walked up through the bushes … and to his surprise, found Casa del Crescendo standing intact.

What the …?

He unlocked the door and switched on the lamp. Everything appeared undamaged, other than just a couple of small cracks in the caulking.

Well, I'll be damned. My humble little shanty came through just fine. All those flashy buildings and structures that were designed and built by high-priced architects and engineers … like Dad … came a-tumbling down. But not Casa del Crescendo.

Once again, he heard his father saying, "Good thing you're a better pianist than carpenter."

Enough of that! Yeah, you're right. I am a better pianist than carpenter. And apparently, I'm not such a bad carpenter. Who knows, maybe I could have been a damn good engineer. I designed and built a structure that stood up to one hell of a hairy earthquake, right down to the tire-strip gaskets between the cinderblocks. I can survive on very little, and I can endure loneliness and rejection. But I won't be humiliated anymore, not by anyone.

"No way I'll quit," he said out loud. "I'm staying. For good."

He returned to his Ford. Reflexively, he reached for his wallet and then remembered. The robbery. Everything taken.

Need to run by the credit union and get some cash. Also, cancel the ATM card. Not much of a chance someone would figure out his PIN, but not impossible, either.

He battled horrendous traffic on both surface streets and the Hollywood Freeway all the way to the Musician's Union. He rushed to the credit union but found it closed.

Crap! I forgot, this is a holiday. MLK day! Probably would have been closed anyway due to the quake. Not good. No wallet, no cash, no ATM card. I have some checks in the storage unit, but there's no way anyone will cash them without some kind of ID.

He pulled out his cell phone and called the after-hours number on the credit union's door. After leaving a message describing the event, he hung up.

See the credit union folks first thing tomorrow morning!

As he finished, his pager buzzed. The readout showed the number for Ed, the composer. He called.

"Hi, Ed, you paged?"

"Sure did," Ed answered. "Crazy day. You okay?"

"I'm fine, thanks. How about you?"

"Fine, thanks. Listen, how soon can you go on the road? Be about a couple of months."

"Uh, well … right away, I guess. What's up?"

"Remember Ben, the guy you subbed for back in August?"

"Sure."

"He's on the road with a young singer. His wife is freaking out over the quake and wants him to come home. Fact is, she wants to dump LA and move back to Dallas right now. The tour will be in Portland tonight. The record company's CEO is flying up there today in his jet. Can you meet him at Van Nuys Airport this afternoon?"

"I … yeah, I guess so." His mind reeled. "I'll need a place to stash my car. My … my pad has on-street parking."

"I'll take care of it for you," Ed told him. "There's a storage yard nearby that doesn't cost too much. Can you meet me at the airport?"

"Sure. I'll head home and pack. Man, I sure owe you."

"Naw, not me. Maury asked for you. He misplaced your card and asked me to call you."

"Good to know. Who's the singer?"

"Young gal named Bobbi Nyland. She's good."

"I know about her. This is great! See you soon."

He almost floated out of the union. This was the best thing to happen to him since he arrived in LA. A *tour*, one with a good steady income for a couple of months. And Maury *asked* for him. No telling how much that could lead to. In the aftermath of a huge earthquake, with all of Los Angeles in chaos, everything seemed to be busting loose for him.

And it was — in part — due to Audrey's chord progressions. I owe her as much as I owe Ed. In spite of all her problems, she still managed to accomplish a hell of a lot in her short life. I'm always saying she "could have been something." Well, bullshit. She WAS something, IS something. Something damn impressive.

He drove back, one last time, to Casa del Crescendo. Westbound traffic on the Ventura Freeway wasn't too bad. Most of the congestion was still in the eastbound direction. He parked in the strip mall lot, put on his hard hat, vest, and glasses, walked down the street … and froze.

At the bottom of the street, next to the gate, he saw a black and white CHP cruiser and an orange Caltrans truck.

Dammit! Not now!

He pondered what to do.

Wait for them to leave?

No. No more hiding. Let's face up to this.

He walked forward and found the gate open. A six-foot-plus CHP officer and a shorter Caltrans worker stood in front of Casa del Crescendo. He took a deep breath and said, "Hello, men."

Both turned and faced him. The Caltrans worker, his old friend Herman, gasped and said, "You?"

"Me."

"Wait," Herman sputtered. "That shed. That's what you built …?"

He nodded and replied, "From the lumber and flakeboard. And some stuff I found dumped on the sides of other highways."

Herman whistled and said, "I'll be damned. That's some good work."

"Thanks. Look guys, I know this is illegal as hell, and I'm sorry. But I just got a fulltime job and came to clear out. Do what you have to do, but if you file charges, I could lose the job and wind up right back where I started."

The CHP officer seemed to glare for a moment, then gave a soft chuckle.

"Relax, no one's getting arrested. We stopped by to see if you were okay. Thing is, we believed that contractor story you told Officer Keegan."

"You did?"

Herman nodded and said, "We all did, up until about a month ago. We had no idea you were a homeless guy. You didn't leave any trash, which is always a dead giveaway. You got rid of the litter and the weeds and saved us some work. It wasn't until one of my guys mentioned you to a friend in our right of way department that we learned there was no contractor here. We decided to let you stay for a little while. Just not indefinitely."

"Thanks. I wasn't planning to stay indefinitely."

"One other thing," the officer said. "You saved us some work, too. You kept other homeless guys out of the area. They constantly bitched about you, and told us *that fucking hardhat guy damn near lives here!*"

The pianist laughed, feeling a wave of relief unlike any he had ever known.

"I appreciate you letting me know this," he told them. "One other thing. I just need my clothes and grooming kit. But the camping equipment belonged to a good guy, an Eagle Scout who died young. The stove's a classic Coleman. See if someone can use it before you toss it."

Herman nodded and said, "I'll do that. Hell, we might even use this shed for storage."

"Hope you do. Oh, and … one more favor. Could you guys keep this whole thing confidential? I'd rather no one ever finds out."

"No problem," Herman said. "So, what's the new job?"

"Two-month road trip with a singer. Bobbi Nyland."

The officer raised his eyebrows in surprise and said, "You're a musician?"

"Pianist," Herman told him. "I've heard him. He's damn good."

The officer grinned and replied, "Touring with Bobbi Nyland. My son will be jealous. He's totally hot for her."

Before heading to the airport, he swung by the storage unit and packed his clothes in an ancient suitcase he'd kept. He wrote a check for two months' worth of rent. Then he dropped off the photos of Casa del Crescendo, his boom box, and his cassette tapes.

No way I'm getting rid of any of these. The bicycle, the boom box and cassette tapes were rejects, other people's discards that nevertheless brought enormous relief and occasional joy. I couldn't have made it without them.

He dropped the check in the manager's mail slot, then drove the Ford out to Van Nuys Airport. After taking the keys to the Ford, Ed introduced him to the CEO of Pacific Records. The CEO, a tall, slender man with piercing grey eyes, shook the pianist's hand and said with a smile, "I'm my own pilot, by the way, so forgive me if I seem to ignore you on this flight."

"Quite all right. Pleasure to be aboard."

Ed told the CEO about the robbery. Then he said to the pianist, "I'll take care of your ATM card tomorrow. How you set on cash?"

"None," he shrugged, embarrassed. "Some pocket change."

Ed reached for his wallet. The CEO stopped him, reached into his wallet and pulled out four twenties.

"This should hold you for a day or two," the CEO told him.

Taking the bills, the pianist said, "Sure will. Thanks. I'll pay you back as soon as I can."

The CEO shook his head and said, "We'll make this is an advance from your first paycheck."

They said goodbye to Ed and walked out across the windy concrete tarmac to the waiting Gulfstream. The pianist settled into a seat and found he was the only passenger. The only other occupants of the cabin were his ancient suitcase and several cardboard boxes full of sheet music.

The CEO closed the cabin door. About twenty minutes later, the Gulfstream roared down the runway and lifted into the sky. A short time later, as Bakersfield passed beneath his window, the pianist started to giggle.

This is ridiculous! A record company CEO is flying a homeless guy aboard his Gulfstream! I may be the only homeless guy in all of history to fly aboard a private jet!

The pianist was glad the cockpit door separated him from the CEO. He couldn't stop laughing at the absurdity of it all. An inner dam had burst, and the giggle-fits poured out of him, unstoppable, impossible to restrain. He laughed and laughed until the Gulfstream passed Fresno, whereupon he fell, exhausted, into the deepest, sweetest sleep he'd known in years.

XI

An hour after landing in Portland, he found himself in a quick rehearsal. The music director, who was none other than Maury's son Jake, had set up the rehearsal for himself, the rhythm section, and Bobbi. She was the last to arrive for the impromptu rehearsal. The pianist saw her and froze.

He'd seen a few pictures of her, but they didn't prepare him for the sight of her in person. Bobbi stood about five nine, had long dark brown hair and enormous dark eyes. She wore sweat pants and a t-shirt and made them look incredibly glamorous.

The first piece of music Jake handed the pianist was "Evermore."

"Pacific likes the song, but didn't care for Tommy's cover," Jake said. "They think it'll work better with a woman."

"Is this the sheet music that came with me?" he asked, forcing himself to look away from her.

Jake nodded and said, "Dad kept your changes, too."

They ran through the tune. Maury and "the suits" at Pacific were right. It worked better as a woman's song, and especially as Bobbi's song. She sounded vulnerable but not needy, passionate but not hysterical. Her phrasing was subtle, but deeply affecting. Unlike many young female singers, who were known mostly for their sultry looks and abbreviated attire, Bobbi knew how to sing. Her voice was strong and flexible, obviously the result of years of voice lessons. She understood phrasing and dynamics.

She could easily get by on her looks. But she's not your average "pop tart." Girl knows what she's doing.

They made one more change to the song. The new ending had Bobbi repeating, "Evermore … evermore … evermore …" as the pianist softly played F-Minor, to B-Diminished, to C-Minor that he held until her voice faded. He held the chord, then dropped his hands. Bobbi rewarded him with a dazzling smile.

That evening, he performed with the orchestra and had to force himself to concentrate on the music and not on Bobbi. The same woman who made a t-shirt and sweat pants look glamorous performed in a sleeveless blouse, a tight, short skirt, and heels. With great determination, he focused his thoughts on the keyboard and Jake, who conducted the orchestra.

Near the end of the performance, she sang "Evermore." The rest of the orchestra remained tacit as he accompanied her. Bobbi sang, "I wonder if you know …" The combination of Audrey's progressions and Bobbi's delicate phrasing provoked quiet gasps from the audience.

The concert ended, and the orchestra rode the bus back to the hotel. After settling in to his room, the pianist experienced a luxury unknown to him for years – an actual bed, one much more luxurious than the spartan hospital bed. He'd become accustomed to his sleeping bag and air mattress, which had been a huge improvement over the front seat of the Falcon. He crawled in and nestled beneath the sheets, and the whole thing felt so damn sumptuous and extravagant – yet he had a tough time falling asleep. He was unaccustomed to such opulence, and felt as if he had no business sleeping in such comfort.

Any moment, the hotel manager could bust open the door and kick your homeless ass the hell out of the room and out onto the street.

Silly, he knew, but he had a tough time shaking the unease and wariness.

Two nights later, while performing in Seattle, he and Bobbi had what can only be described as … A Moment. She sang, "I hope you don't know," and he played the F7 to E-Flat Minor …

And … they spoke without speaking. They touched without touching. For one brief but unforgettable moment, they occupied the same space. A million clichés have been coined to describe that moment, none of them completely accurate, none of them completely wrong. But he felt it, and was sure she did, too. He suspected the others in the orchestra may have felt the vibe between the two of them. Perhaps even a few people in the audience sensed it.

Later, after everyone returned to the hotel, he took the elevator down to the first floor and asked concierge, "Is the ballroom open?"

"No. Ms. Nyland asked us to keep it closed. She wants to practice piano for a while."

She plays piano, too? I shouldn't be surprised.

"Thanks."

As he walked down to the ballroom, he heard the familiar sound of the Hanon exercises. He tried the door and found it was unlocked. Opening it, he entered the ballroom and closed the door behind him as quietly as possible.

She finished the exercise, and he said, "Ms. Nyland?"

He did not startle her at all. She turned around, almost as if she had been expecting him.

"Hello," she said with a captivating smile. "What brings you here?"

"The desk told me you were practicing. I won't keep you from that. But I just wanted to tell you how much I've enjoyed working with you."

"Thank you. You're a wonderful accompanist. I'd like to hear you as a soloist someday."

"Thanks."

"Please, sit down," she said.

"Sure? I don't want to bother you."

"You're not bothering me."

They made small talk for a few minutes. He told her about his days at the Cincinnati Conservatory, and the year at Berklee in Boston. She told him about her undergrad days at UCLA studying Public Policy, and how a talent agent heard her sing at an open mike in Santa Monica.

"I feel silly sometime," she said. "So many singers struggle for years. I just fell into this."

"It's not silly," he told her. "You've got the talent, and you've obviously put in the work."

They both knew they were circling each other, stalling, and avoiding the obvious. At last she gazed at him and half-whispered, "Did you … feel that tonight?"

"Sure did."

They stood, embraced, and kissed, softly at first, then passionately. He wasn't used to kissing a woman who matched his height. But he quickly decided he liked it. After several wonderful long moments, they paused and drew apart.

"Are we insane? So quickly?" she murmured.

"No," he answered. "Makes total sense. But there's something I should tell you. Let's sit down."

He told her everything. The months of living in the Ford, then building and living in Casa del Crescendo.

"Wow," she said. "That's … some story."

"Listen, if it's a deal-breaker, I'll understand."

She smiled and shook her head.

"It's not a deal-breaker. Just the opposite. It's impressive. Not many people could survive all that."

His heart pounded.

"You mean it?"

"I mean it."

"Bobbi —"

She placed her index finger on his lips.

"One thing. I'd rather you call me Roberta."

"Of course."

"Bobbi is the name the record company came up with. They want a proper name for a sexy young airhead."

"You're not … an airhead," he told her.

She smiled. They kissed again. Then she took his hand and whispered, "Let's go."

The two of them were inseparable for the rest of the tour. When it finished, she offered to let him move in with her. But he told her he wanted his own place one last time, if only to prove to himself that he could pay for his own housing, just like everyone else. She understood, and after six months of his living in a sublet Fountain Avenue apartment, just north of the union, they moved in together. A few months later, they married.

Gigs started to come more frequently. Ed hired him for another film score session, and for the recording of the theme music for a television series pilot that, unfortunately, never sold. Maury called him for another recording session with Tommy Hartrick, and for another couple of unknown young singers.

Shortly after he moved in with Roberta, he called his sister and told her, "Listen, there's something I need to tell you."

He confessed the entire story of his homeless period, both the time living in the Ford and in Casa del Crescendo. His sister listened without comment. When he finished, she told him, "I'd pretty much guessed most of it."

"You did?"

"Yeah. I first started to suspect it when you told me to send your mail to the post office. You never mentioned any sort of room or apartment or roommate. Sometimes it was just the tone of your voice. But why didn't you ask me for help?"

"I was ... too embarrassed," he said. "Didn't want to be a burden."

After "Evermore" became a hit, Roberta recorded one more album. One year after the first tour, she embarked on another, this one to promote her newest work. Once again, he joined the orchestra. The tour brought in another two months' work of income. But despite critical praise, none of the songs charted. The CEO – the one who flew the Gulfstream — either retired or was forced out. The new man in charge at Pacific dropped her contract.

Rather than trying to sign with a new record label, Roberta took her pop diva money, finished her Public Policy degree, and then enrolled in UCLA Law School, studying entertainment law. She took a position with an up-and-coming LA firm and made a career of fighting record companies, including Pacific Records. In her spare time she helped him set up a program with the union that offered discrete assistance to homeless musicians.

Unlike many other musicians' marriages, theirs not only endured, it blossomed. He became a sought-after recording session pianist. Every

Wednesday night, he performed with a trio at The Boiler Room, the site of his ill-fated gig with Chucky Betts. Roberta often sat in with him.

He recorded a jazz album that featured Roberta on three of the songs. Maury produced the album and offered superb guidance. His old friend Skip played drums. The album sold surprisingly well and made the Billboard chart for jazz releases.

"You're the reason the album is selling any copies at all," he told her.

"Come on," she laughed. "I'm a has-been. No one remembers me."

"Sure they do."

He sold the Ford to his friend Andy, the Ferrari dealer he'd met at the Holmby Hills wedding reception, and found no small measure of amusement at the joy a high-end car dealer took in an unsexy old Falcon Ranchero. Again and again, Andy gushed, "It's totally original! Perfect! Perfect!" The little Ford had a good, loving home.

Instead of buying a flashy new car, the pianist tracked down his old Toyota. The man who bought it from him still owned it. After some quick negotiating, they settled on a deal. He drove the Toyota home with an idiotic sense of triumph and redemption.

He kept his Panasonic bike, even when other cyclists told him it was outdated. Riley overhauled it with another new chain and cassette, new tires, wheels, and brakes. The pianist rode almost every day and came to rely on the peace of mind the rides provided. Soon, Roberta bought her own bike and joined him on the early morning rounds.

Just about every relationship counselor, every amateur expert, every locker room friend says the same thing: Never tell your current girlfriend or wife the details about a previous relationship. They want to think they are the first women you really cared about.

He supposed there was some truth to that. And he supposed men were just as insecure. They probably didn't want to hear about some old boyfriend.

But he wanted to be completely honest with Roberta about everything. And he knew Roberta was far too mature and self-confident to dissolve into childish tantrums over an ex-girlfriend. One night he sat down with her, told her about Audrey, and played the Sonata in C-Minor for her.

"Beautiful piece," Roberta told him.

"Yeah. But Audrey was right," he said. "We were too different to be a long-term couple. It couldn't last."

"Did you know she was a lesbian?"

"No. According to her girlfriend, Audrey didn't know, either."

"She sounds … kind of eccentric."

He nodded and said, "You'll find other musicians like her. Brilliant at music, clueless about life."

She sighed and said, "I've already met them."

"Most people only see the cluelessness. They don't get the genius. Thing is … I know you get it."

Roberta offered a sad smile.

"She deserved a longer life."

"She did."

Three years after they married, Roberta accompanied him on a return trip to the Cincinnati Conservatory. He and Doc Deegan arranged a tribute to Audrey.

He met Deegan in the familiar old office and found a stout woman with short brown hair sitting in a leather chair. She wore metal, Vince Lombardi-style glasses.

"I'm Alice Wintermantel," she said in her charcoal voice.

"Honored to meet you," he replied. "Thanks for helping us with the program."

That evening, he played several of Audrey's compositions, including her Sonata in C-Minor and her Piano Concerto in A-Major, the latter accompanied by the Conservatory Orchestra. When the program ended, he found himself back in the familiar rehearsal hall-turned-reception room, where once again Doc Deegan's wife served her famous punch to the guests. He stood in a reception line, greeting many familiar faces, including Haynes D'Arcineau, the famous music critic.

At one point, Alice Wintermantel greeted him.

"Someone I'd like you to meet," he told her. He motioned for Roberta to join him.

"This is Roberta."

Alice and Roberta shook hands. Roberta said, "Thank you for preserving Audrey's work. She was brilliant."

Alice gave a brittle nod and said, "Thank you. Audrey deserved this night."

For the most part, he avoided the Ventura Freeway on ramp that hosted Casa del Crescendo. He looked back on those bleak days with distaste, and certainly had no desire to revisit that chapter.

But one day in 2001, he dropped Ed, the composer, off at Burbank Airport. As he drove west on the Ventura Freeway back to his new home in Woodland Hills, curiosity got the best of him. He took the old exit, crossed under the overpass and parked his beloved Toyota in the strip mall parking lot. The hair salon, pet food store, and insurance agency were still in business.

Just one week before, he read an article in the LA Times about celebrities who had endured periods of homelessness. The article named several actors and singers, some of whom he had come to know. None seemed ashamed of the experience. Some regarded it as a badge of honor, indisputable proof of their dogged determination to make it in LA. He thought about the others, Hollywood's anonymous artists and technicians who also found themselves homeless – the film editors, art directors, sound designers, studio musicians – and wondered if they felt the same way.

He'd told only four people – his sister, Roberta, Herman and the CHP officer. He knew Roberta and his sister would never tell, and instinctively knew Herman and the cop would keep their word. In the years since, not one person he worked with ever told him they were on to his secret, or even hinted as much, and he was happy with that.

He thought of the lyrics from "Evermore."

"I wonder if you know …"

He walked down the road, and up the side of the church parking lot until he found the end of the fence. He climbed over the fence and saw no bushes, weeds or grass, just barren soil beneath the few remaining trees. No doubt the landscaping fell victim to both budget cutbacks and the ongoing drought. He reversed direction and walked back to where the shed used to be. He found no trace of Casa del Crescendo. Nothing. Even the cinderblock foundations had vanished.

He paced around the dry soil.

All gone. No physical evidence left. But that's good, that's the way I want it.

"I'll never let you know …"

His life in the shed had been miserable. He hated the constant hiding, the lying, the ever-present fear of being discovered and humiliated. Yet now, with all traces gone, he felt an odd sense of loss, as if something of value had been taken from him. The only remaining evidence of the shed's existence lay in the yellowing photos he had snapped with the disposable camera.

It was a lousy time. Yet … I built a shelter out of other people's worthless discards and detritus. And my little shanty stood up to one of the worst earthquakes to ever hit California.

Maybe they're onto something. Maybe those of us who survived homelessness have a right to feel proud. If not proud, at least not ashamed. Roberta told me as much that night in Seattle. I'm not going to volunteer any of this. I won't go blabbing about it to People Magazine or Entertainment Tonight. But if anyone ever finds out, I won't deny it. No reason to. Not anymore.

He returned to the street, got back in his car and drove down the road, beneath the underpass. Turning left, he accelerated up the onramp, onto the westbound Ventura Freeway and into the evening traffic, with the red California sunset guiding him home.

Author's Note

Two of the plot devices in this story were inspired by the work of others, and I wish to express my gratitude.

The four-bar chord progression from Audrey's "Sonata in C-Minor," and later used in "Evermore," comes from the song "Recessional" by Vienna Teng. The progression is at the :40 and 1:36 marks. Vienna graciously granted her permission to incorporate the progression into the narrative. In my thoroughly un-humble opinion, she is the most brilliant singer-songwriter of our time.

In 2015, while working for the California Department of Transportation, I took part in a homeless encampment sweep in San Jose. Among the usual tents I found a person living in an enclosed lean-to. Although the construction details differ – this lean-to was, if I recall correctly, sheathed in cardboard – the basic design of that structure served as a spark for this story. I sincerely hope the person who built that shelter has since found better living conditions.

Oakland, California
February, 2024